"You don't have to do that, Miss O'Dell." *Everett's tone sounded brittle. "This isn't the hotel dining room."*

Tillie froze in her tracks with a stack of dishes in her hands. Was this the same arrogance and disdain he'd extended to her the day he discovered she worked as a waitress at the hotel? Her Irish temper flared in her chest, but she immediately suppressed it.

"Everett." Hubert stood and cast an apologetic look at Tillie. "Don't be boorish."

Tillie willed her hands not to tremble. "It's all right." Her voice was so hushed she almost couldn't hear it herself. Her father's favorite verse and gentle admonition ran through her head. *"Be ye kind one to another, tenderhearted, forgiving one another. . . ."* It wasn't Everett's fault. They'd practically forced him into spending the afternoon with her. He wasn't used to being around people since the fire. She'd grown up watching people react to her father's scars—the looks of pity, horror, and repulsion.

"I apologize, Everett, if I've offended you in any way. Please forgive me."

CONNIE STEVENS lives in north Georgia with her husband of over thirty-five years, John. She and John are active in a variety of capacities in their home church. One cantankerous kitty—misnamed Sweet Pea—allows them to live in her home. Some of Connie's favorite pastimes include reading, sewing, browsing antique shops, collecting teddy bears, and gardening. She also enjoys making quilts to send to the Cancer Treatment Center of America. Visit Connie's website and blog at www. conniestevenswrites.com.

Books by Connie Stevens

HEARTSONG PRESENTS
HP936—Leave Me Never
HP951—Revealing Fire

Don't miss out on any of our super romances. Write to us at the following address for information on our newest releases and club information.

Heartsong Presents Readers' Service
PO Box 721
Uhrichsville, OH 44683

Or visit www.heartsongpresents.com

Scars of Mercy

Connie Stevens

Heartsong Presents

To Suze:
Thanks for being there when I needed you.

A note from the Author:
I love to hear from my readers! You may correspond with me by writing:

Connie Stevens
Author Relations
PO Box 721
Uhrichsville, OH 44683

ISBN 978-1-61626-446-8

SCARS OF MERCY

All scripture quotations are taken from the King James Version of the Bible.

This book is a work of fiction. Names, characters, places, and incidents are either products of the author's imagination or used fictitiously.

Our mission is to publish and distribute inspirational products offering exceptional value and biblical encouragement to the masses.

PRINTED IN THE U.S.A.

one

Willow Creek, Iowa, 1885

Everett Behr shot a scowl of self-loathing at his reflection in the hand mirror. If it weren't for having to shave, he might well refuse to own a mirror. With cautious, deliberate strokes, he drew the razor around the scars along his jawline on the right side of his face. He'd hoped a thick crop of whiskers would hide the scars. He couldn't abide the stares, however sympathetic. They only served to remind him that the price of his arrogance would be forever branded across his face. Much to his frustration, his beard grew in patches, refusing to sprout in the scarred areas he most wanted to hide. The fragments of whiskers popping out in an irregular, crazy quilt pattern surrounded the scars instead of covering them, as if framing the ugliness for display.

He wiped the last of the shaving soap from his face just as the bell on the little church at the end of the street began calling the people of Willow Creek to worship. Everett didn't hurry. Attending church services meant doing so on his terms. Accepting his scars was one thing, and he wanted to know more about the God who'd allowed them. He just didn't relish mingling with people before or after the service.

He turned the mirror glass-side down on the washstand and released an involuntary huff. With practiced fingers, he tied his cravat and combed his hair—grateful he could perform those duties by feel rather than by sight.

By the time the church bell stopped clanging, Everett knew

most of the congregation had entered the building and taken their seats. With curious eyes now safely confined within the walls of the church, Everett picked up his Bible and prepared to walk to the church and slip in unnoticed.

He descended the recently completed back steps that afforded him a private entrance to the living quarters over the mercantile his father owned. In the past several months he'd memorized every alley and wooded path so he could avoid walking down the town boardwalk whenever possible.

A squirrel chattered from a nearby tree, scolding Everett for disturbing his breakfast. Digging into his pocket, Everett withdrew a few peanuts and held them aloft. "Here's your treat, little buddy." He tossed the peanuts at the base of the tree from which the squirrel regarded him, now with less animosity. But the little creature switched his bushy tail back and forth like the lash of a buggy whip and refused to come closer until Everett backed off.

"All right, I don't blame you. Nobody else wants to come near me either." A twinge of guilt over his self-pity pricked him. He should be grateful to be alive. Everett turned and proceeded toward the church. By the time he reached the edge of the churchyard, the sounds of the hymn-singing beckoned him to draw near the little house of worship. He hoped he'd find a seat at the back near the door.

The congregation's enthusiastic praise rang within the walls of the church as he opened the door just enough to step inside. It didn't seem to matter to these people that their church had no stained-glass windows, thick carpeting, or ornately carved pews. They raised their voices to God as though they stood in a magnificent cathedral.

"How firm a foundation, ye saints of the Lord, is laid for your faith in His excellent Word." Everett's heart started singing along with the congregation in praise to his newfound Lord.

He closed the door silently and took his place on the bench against the back wall. No heads turned, no pitiful or repulsed looks greeted him. Everett relaxed. The hymn ended, and the congregation sat. Everett opened his Bible, being careful to turn the pages quietly.

Looking over the backs of the heads in front of him, he located Father with his new bride. Hubert and Pearl Behr sat in the second row near the aisle. When Pearl leaned closer to his father as they shared one Bible, Everett berated himself again for his past misguided efforts to separate the two. Pearl was a good woman, and she made his father happy.

Across the aisle from Father and Pearl, Tillie O'Dell sat with her family. Her dark blond hair, pinned up and secured with a green ribbon, gleamed in the morning sun streaming through the window. A memory teased his subconscious. The afternoon he'd spent with Tillie last year at a church picnic wafted across his mind like a gentle breeze. He shook himself and pushed the picture away. That was a lifetime ago—before the fire that left his face and hands mottled with ugly scars. No sense in entertaining thoughts now far beyond the reach of reality. Even if his face, neck, and hands weren't scarred, the disdain with which he'd treated Tillie a week after the picnic when he learned she worked in the hotel dining room ensured she'd want nothing to do with him.

Everett pulled his attention back to the sermon. Deep in his heart he wanted to know how God could use him. Could God take a broken and marred vessel like him and remake it into something good? Doubts pricked him, but he listened intently anyway, hoping to grab on to some fleeting comment from the pastor—anything to give him a glimmer of worthiness.

He followed along as the pastor read the scripture and made a notation in the margin of his Bible in preparation to return to the passage later and study it in depth. But his attention kept drifting to the back of Tillie's head. Something within him kept tugging at his mind, a futile wish to turn back the calendar and recant his arrogance. He supposed nobody lived without some regrets of one type or another, but his behavior had hurt people he cared about.

The singing of the congregation startled him. He'd been so lost in his own brooding, he'd missed the rest of the sermon. Heat crept into his face, even though he was relatively sure his presence at the back of the room had gone unnoticed. He stood and slipped out the door, hurrying down the steps before the people began spilling out of the church.

Halfway across the churchyard, he heard a familiar voice call out his name.

"Everett! Wait, son."

He welcomed the pleasure of his father's company, but he'd rather choose a less public place. Stepping into the shadow of the thick cedar trees that lined the churchyard and casting self-conscious glances around him, he waited for his father and Pearl to approach.

"We weren't sure you were coming to church this morning, son." His father extended his hand and clasped Everett's.

Pearl reached out and touched his arm. "We'd be pleased if you'd join us for Sunday dinner." Her blue eyes twinkled. "I suspect that you're partial to my chicken and dumplings, since you asked for seconds the last time I made them."

Everett's mouth watered. He'd never tasted anything quite as good as the simple, hearty dishes Pearl served at her table. Even the fancy beef roasts and lobster on which he'd dined while growing up in his grandparents' home couldn't compare to Pearl's chicken and dumplings.

The rest of the congregation milled about the churchyard, shaking hands with the pastor and visiting with each other.

If he wished to escape their scrutinizing stares, he needed to give Pearl an answer.

"I would enjoy that. Thank you for the invitation."

"This way, son. Our wagon is over by those cottonwoods." Father placed a tender hand on Pearl's back and led the way to the conveyance. Just as Everett started after them, another voice hailed him.

"Everett? Everett Behr."

His feet froze momentarily. The unmistakable lilt identified the voice as belonging to Tillie O'Dell. Two other times in recent weeks she'd called out to him in the churchyard, but he'd pretended not to hear. No longer the same man with whom she'd spent a carefree afternoon almost a year ago, he couldn't face her. Even if he wanted to apologize for snubbing her, the fingerprint left by the flames on his face and hands made him wish he could duck into a cave somewhere and never emerge again. He forced his feet to move rapidly toward his father's market wagon.

☙

Tillie O'Dell plunked her hands on her hips and heaved an exasperated sigh as she watched Everett hasten away. Goodness, that man was as elusive as a will-o'-the-wisp. She hurried to help Ma gather her younger siblings into their family's farm wagon and then turned toward her father, who was checking a hoof on one of the horses.

"Da?"

He dropped the hoof and straightened. The moment he fixed his gaze on her, merriment danced in his eyes. "Lass, you look like a cat preying on a sparrow."

She pressed her lips together. No use trying to fool Da. His sage insight pierced right through her. "Would it be all right if I go talk to Everett Behr?"

Da glanced across the churchyard, where Everett was

climbing into the back of the wagon his father used to make deliveries from the mercantile. A wistful expression came over her father's face as he ran one finger over the scar that carved a ragged furrow from the bridge of his nose to his ear—an unconscious gesture she'd seen her father do from time to time, usually when he was contemplating something. If he had any misgivings about her spending time with Everett, he'd say so. Instead he gave her a nod, and she could have sworn she caught a glimpse of a smile.

"Thanks, Da. Don't bother waiting for me. It's a delightful day for a walk." With lifted chin, she scurried across the yard before the Behrs' wagon left.

As she approached, she caught Pearl Behr's eye. The sweet, gray-haired woman sent her a warm smile and then flicked her gaze over her shoulder where Everett settled himself behind the bench seat. Taking the welcoming smile as encouragement, Tillie walked up to the wagon and drew in a deep breath.

"Hello, Miss Pearl, Mr. Behr. . .Everett. How are all of you this morning?"

"Hello, Miss Tillie." Hubert Behr's mustache always jiggled when he smiled and spoke at the same time. "Fine Lord's morning, isn't it?"

From the corner of her eye, she saw Everett hunch his shoulders and pull his collar up despite the warm sunshine. His left hand slid toward his face, and he turned away from her. A pang of sadness twisted within her, and she wished Everett weren't so self-conscious of the scars he had sustained in the fire.

"Yes, it's a lovely day. Don't you think so, Everett?" She'd use whatever means at hand to engage Everett in conversation, even a trivial discussion of the day's weather. To her dismay, Everett merely shrugged a noncommittal response and tugged his broad-brimmed hat a bit lower. Clearly she needed to come to the point. She sucked in another deep breath to fortify her waning courage and plunged ahead.

"Everett, I've been trying to speak with you for weeks now, but every time I see you, you hurry away. Is there some reason you don't wish to talk to me?" She waited to see if her boldness might loosen his tongue.

"I apologize, Miss Tillie. I didn't mean to be rude. . . ." Everett's mumbled reply from behind his hand barely reached her ears.

"Tillie, won't you join us for Sunday dinner?" Miss Pearl's graciousness made Tillie's heart speed up and her cheeks grow warm. She hadn't been fishing for an invitation to dinner, but if it meant spending the afternoon with Everett, the prospect sent a tingle all the way to her toes.

"Why, that's so kind of you, Miss Pearl. I'd love to."

Everett jerked his head toward his stepmother. The expression on his face—either anger or panic, she couldn't tell which—pulled his mouth into a frown. For a split second, she thought maybe Miss Pearl might rescind the invitation, but she didn't, and Tillie's acceptance put a smile on the woman's face, if not on Everett's.

Since Everett made no move to help her climb into the wagon, Tillie turned with her back to the wagon and placed both palms on the edge of the tailgate, hoisting herself up. She tucked her feet beneath her to steady herself and scooted back farther into the wagon bed. Not a very ladylike maneuver, to be sure, but since Everett chose to leave her to her own devices, she scrambled aboard the best she could. Once seated across from him, she primly arranged her skirt to cover her ankles. With teeth clamped together, she forced a smile and willed herself not to make mention of Everett's lack of gallantry.

"Everybody set? Let's go. I can smell the chicken and dumplings from here." Mr. Behr released the brake and slapped the reins on the horse's back. The lurching motion of the wagon caught Tillie off balance, and she careened into Everett's shoulder. His hand flew out to catch her, but he immediately snatched it back.

"Oh, I'm sorry." Telltale heat climbed up her neck, and her mind raced to remember which of Everett's arms was burned. "Did I hurt you?"

Everett glared at her from under the brim of his hat. "No harm done," he mumbled, and shifted his position until she could barely see even the unblemished half of his face.

Tillie brushed an errant strand of hair from her face. "I missed seeing you in church. I was hoping I could speak with you before the service."

A soft huff defined Everett's opinion of her attempt at conversation. "I arrived late."

"Oh." She waited to see if he would elaborate. He didn't. "You know, my Ma and I made a huge batch of Irish soda bread yesterday. I just love it with fresh currant jelly. I should have brought you some. Perhaps Miss Pearl and Mr. Hubert might enjoy some as well. As soon as the currants are ripe for picking, I'll bring you a jar of jelly. With six brothers and sisters, we certainly go through a lot of jam and jelly at our house. My brother Phillip can eat almost a whole loaf of bread by himself if he has a jar of jelly at hand. Ma and I just finished putting up a double batch of strawberry jam, and the blackberries should be ready in a few weeks. Do you—"

Everett cleared his throat. "That's fine, Miss Tillie. I'm sure Father and Pearl would appreciate it."

Too late she remembered her Da's twinkling eyes when he teased her. *"Don't know of another female who can outchatter a magpie like our Matilda."* Clearly Everett wasn't inclined to engage in small talk. Either she could carry the conversation, or they could sit in uncomfortable silence.

Perhaps silence wasn't uncomfortable to Everett. Growing up in a houseful of noisy children, with a blarney-filled father and a mother who liked to sing while she worked, the O'Dell house was never quiet. She didn't even know if Everett had siblings.

They rode the rest of the way to the Behr house without any further attempts on her part to coax Everett into talking. Tillie studied his profile—what she could see of it. His hat brim shadowed his brow and eyes, but the corner of his mouth bore a distinct downturn, evidence that he wasn't happy being stuck with her company. If he remained in such a sullen mood, a very long afternoon threatened to stretch out before her.

two

Tillie set a china bowl of green beans on the linen-covered table and sneaked a glance from the dining room into the living area. Everett and his father sat across from each other in large leather chairs in front of the fireplace. She'd caught the grimace in Everett's expression when they stepped into the Behrs' house and he had to remove his hat. He'd seemed relieved when she offered to help in the kitchen. Pearl set the tureen of chicken and dumplings on the table and called to the men. Everett hesitated, and Tillie could only guess by his reticence that he was trying to think of a way to excuse himself and leave.

Instead he walked into the dining room and held Tillie's chair for her before seating himself to her right. She thanked him, her face warming at his polite gesture. As soon as they were all seated, Hubert held out his hands, one to Pearl and one to Everett.

"Let's join hands and pray."

Join hands? Well, of course they held hands at home when Da offered the blessing at mealtime. He always teased that it was to keep the boys from snitching his portion of the food while his head was bowed. But now, Hubert and Pearl were waiting for Everett to take Tillie's hand. She could feel his reluctance hanging like a thick fog in the space between them.

After several seconds, Everett extended his hand. The moment their fingers touched, her breath caught in her throat. How to describe such magic? Is this what a dove felt when it took flight? Did a butterfly know this exhilaration after it struggled free of its cocoon and spread its wings for the first time?

Guilt pricked her as her attention fled from Hubert's prayer. Could Everett hear her heart pounding? When Hubert's rumbling voice pronounced the amen, Everett instantly dropped her hand. But the magic remained, and she had to remind herself to breathe normally.

It occurred to her that from this angle, she couldn't tell the flames ever touched him unless he turned his head toward her, which he didn't. Perhaps that was why he'd held her chair—to ensure she wouldn't be able to see his scars from where she sat. A pang arrowed through her, and she searched for a definition. It wasn't pity. . . . No, it was more like sorrow that Everett felt he had to go to such lengths to hide his scars.

"Everett, would you like a roll?" Pearl picked up the bread basket and held it out to him.

He started to accept the basket with his right hand but quickly switched. "Thank you." He set the basket down, took a roll, and deposited it on his plate; then he picked up the basket with his left hand again and passed it to her. Watching Everett maneuver reminded Tillie of attempting to cross a swiftly running stream, jumping from rock to rock, trying not to get wet. She suddenly realized his tactics were because of her presence. Surely he wasn't this self-conscious around Hubert and Pearl. Perhaps it was time for some maneuvering of her own.

"Everything is so delicious, Miss Pearl." Tillie scooped a small second helping of chicken and dumplings from the tureen onto her plate. "These dumplings are as light as an angel's wing."

"Why, thank you, Tillie. For compliments like that, I'll just have to invite you to dinner more often." Pearl chuckled and passed the butter to Hubert.

"And how would you know how much an angel's wing weighs?"

Everett's question took her so by surprise she assumed he was teasing, and she laughed with delight at the thought of him joking with her. But Everett didn't laugh. Tillie swallowed back the giggle and coughed to cover the sound.

"I must admit I don't have any idea how much an angel's wing weighs. It's just an expression my Da uses."

Hubert chuckled. "I've heard some of Timothy O'Dell's Irish expressions. That man could charm a smile from the grumpiest person in town." He blotted his mouth with his napkin. "Timothy came in the store the other day and asked if I sold slippers for wee folk. I thought he was talking about one of his little girls, that cute little one. . .the one with the freckles and pigtails. What is her name?"

Tillie laughed. "That would be Brenna, but Brenna is not wee folk."

Hubert shook his head and laughed again. "That father of yours sure had me going. He kept showing me, like so"—he held his thumb and forefinger two inches apart—"how small the slippers needed to be, and he was quite adamant they had to be green. I was checking the catalog to see if I could order slippers that tiny. He finally told me that *wee folk* are—"

"Leprechauns." Tillie grinned. "Da loves to tease."

Hubert and Pearl both enjoyed the amusing story, and Tillie watched Everett for some indication of a smile, but there was none. She reflected back to the afternoon she'd spent with Everett at the church picnic a year ago, before he was burned, and pictured his warm, engaging smile. She wished to see it again.

"I suppose"—she glanced at Everett and winced inwardly

to see the frown still in place—"I should yield to Everett's challenge and admit I was stretching my description of your dumplings, Miss Pearl, since no one can measure the lightness of an angel's wing."

Everett shrugged. "I didn't mean to insult." A barely audible huff blew past his lips, and he pushed his plate away.

Tillie forced a small laugh. "No offense taken." How hard must one work at being so surly? While it sorrowed her heart to think of the drastic change the fire had caused in Everett's personality, a part of her bristled. She felt like shaking the young man and informing him that he wasn't the only person who'd ever experienced pain or adversity. She nibbled on a few more bites of dumpling. God didn't make mistakes, and she was quite certain she'd felt His nudge, but this man was mighty pigheaded.

A three-way conversation continued over the meal. Everett's lack of participation rang hollow in Tillie's ears. Within her spirit, she conceded to her disappointed anticipation. After enough time elapsed that the remainder of food on his plate must have surely grown cold, Everett pushed back his chair and stood. "Forgive me, I'm afraid I'm not very good company."

"Oh, Everett, you can't go yet," Pearl declared. "I've made a gingerbread cake for dessert."

Hubert flapped his hand, motioning for Everett to sit. "Please stay, son."

Tillie rose. "Yes, Everett, please stay." She glanced at Hubert and Pearl for support. "Why don't I help you clear the table, Miss Pearl, and let these two catch up on their man-talk." She began picking up plates and flatware to carry to the kitchen.

"You don't have to do that, Miss O'Dell." Everett's tone sounded brittle. "This isn't the hotel dining room."

Tillie froze in her tracks with a stack of dishes in her hands. Was this the same arrogance and disdain he'd extended to her the day he discovered she worked as a waitress at the hotel? Her Irish temper flared in her chest, but she immediately suppressed it.

"Everett." Hubert stood and cast an apologetic look at Tillie. "Don't be boorish."

Tillie willed her hands not to tremble. "It's all right." Her voice was so hushed she almost couldn't hear it herself. Her father's favorite verse and gentle admonition ran through her head. *"Be ye kind one to another, tenderhearted, forgiving one another. . . ."* It wasn't Everett's fault. They'd practically forced him into spending the afternoon with her. He wasn't used to being around people since the fire. She'd grown up watching people react to her father's scars—the looks of pity, horror, and repulsion.

"I apologize, Everett, if I've offended you in any way. Please forgive me." She hurried to the kitchen with the stack of dishes.

Before she could deposit the china on the work counter, Everett followed her. "Miss O'Dell. . .Tillie, I'm sorry. I didn't mean that the way it sounded. I just meant that you're a guest, and you shouldn't have to do those things."

As soon as she turned to face him, he averted his gaze and drew his left hand up, his fingers covering his right jawline. Da always said a person's eyes and expression could be read like a book to see what was going on in their heart. But Everett's expression was unreadable, especially when he kept turning away from her.

She returned her attention to scraping the dishes. "I don't mind helping. It makes me feel useful. Being a guest is too stiff and formal for me." She paused, her back still to him. "Everett, I'm sorry, too. I didn't stop to think that being with people might be uncomfortable for you."

She heard him sigh. "I suppose I'll have to get used to it."

Tillie started to turn, and Everett slipped his hand back up to his face. "Everett, a man is made up of what's on the inside."

"Yes, well, that's easy for you to say. You're—"

When she turned to see why he didn't finish his sentence, Everett spun on his heel and strode out of the kitchen.

"I'm what?" She pondered the question. Curiosity pricked her to hear him finish his thought, but underlying misgiving prevented her from following after him to ask what it was he had been about to say.

❧

Everett laid down his fork. Half of his dessert sat untouched on his plate. Normally he devoured Pearl's gingerbread cake, but today it went down like sawdust. He took a swallow of coffee.

Hubert cleared his throat. "The crops look good this year. If the weather holds, there will be plenty to celebrate come harvesttime."

Tillie nodded. "Da says he expects a bumper crop of corn and beans. Even Ma's kitchen garden is keeping her busy with canning. Has there been any discussion of the annual harvest picnic? I realize it's early yet—harvest won't take place for another three months, so there is ample time to plan."

Everett's senses went on alert at Tillie's question. Apparently the picnic was some sort of tradition every autumn. While Tillie and Pearl chatted about the possibilities of having a pie-eating contest and apple bobbing at this year's event, Everett wished he could think of a way to excuse himself and hurry back to his living quarters over the mercantile. He didn't intend to participate in the celebration, even if it was still three months away. His devised method of slipping into church unnoticed after the service began and leaving ahead of the rest of the congregation allowed him to attend worship in relative comfort. Lingering after the services to fellowship with folks didn't appeal to him in the least. He had no intention of giving people the opportunity to gawk.

"What do you think, Everett?" Tillie's soft voice tickled his ears, and he almost turned his head in her direction.

"About what?"

Tillie shook her head. "Pfft! Just like a man. Cogitating on things instead of paying attention to what my Da calls 'women's frivolities.' But he just says that to agitate Ma. He has more fun at the picnics than the children do."

Tilting his head just enough to see her from the corner of his eye was a mistake. Her smile lit up the room. Why did she have to smile like that? Just when he'd settled into his grumpy disposition, wishing she would mind her own business and leave him alone, the sound of her laughter and her sparkling green eyes chipped away at his defenses.

The heat that rose from his belly and upward into his face tingled the scars along his jawline. He gritted his teeth and stiffened his spine. "Why should I pay attention to a discussion that doesn't concern me?"

Tillie's face reddened. "I just thought. . .that is, I hoped. . ." Everett watched her slide her gaze to Pearl, and she appeared to be silently asking for help. Guilt smote Everett. He'd been asking God to help him break down his arrogant demeanor and replace it with kindness. Clearly he still needed more work.

Hubert broke in. "The harvest picnic is something the whole town looks forward to. It's a time when we all come together as a big family and celebrate the way God has blessed us. Why don't you ladies speak to Pastor and Mrs. Witherspoon about it?" He patted his stomach. "Pearl, my love, you've done it again. I'm so full I can hardly move." He rose and pushed his chair back. "I'm going to see if I can walk off some of this dinner. Everett, come and keep me company."

Everett rose and readily joined his father. At least it would get him out of the house and away from Tillie. Dodging her attempts at conversation as well as maneuvering so she couldn't stare at him wore him out. "Yes, I believe I will. Thank you for dinner, Pearl. It was delicious. If you will excuse us." He sent a curt nod in Tillie's direction. He didn't wish to be rude, especially since she was only trying to be nice. But he didn't need anyone going out of their way to demonstrate pity.

He followed his father out to the front porch and down the steps. Pearl had planted a variety of colorful flowers along the front of the house. He had to admit that between the flower beds outside and the curtains and cushions inside, the place did look more inviting. His father's house had been the grateful recipient of a woman's touch.

A woman's touch. The very idea seared his heart much like the flames had tracked their fingerprints across his face. No woman would want to make a life with him. Not even Tillie. Why did she keep trying to pull him into a conversation?

He sucked in a breath of fresh air, free of the encumbrances of trying to hide his scars. His father turned wisdom-filled eyes on him.

"You looked like you needed an escape."

Mottled skin pulled when he smiled. "You're very insightful. Tillie is a nice girl, but having people stare at me is quite uncomfortable."

"Tillie wasn't staring at you."

Everett snorted. "Only because I stayed in constant motion trying to outmaneuver her. I'm exhausted."

Even without looking at his father, Everett could hear the smile in his voice. "Maybe you should stop running and let her catch you."

Surely Father was joking. He didn't plan to dignify the jest with an answer. Instead he changed the subject.

"I finally received a letter last Friday from Grandfather's lawyer." He sighed. "If you'll recall, last year Grandfather's business went into receivership. Thankfully, all the creditors have now been paid."

Father walked silently beside him as they headed toward a stand of poplars. He'd have to break the news eventually. Might as well be now when there was nobody else around to overhear.

"The money that was left is a small fraction of what I'd expected." He adjusted his lapels and the silk cravat at his throat. "I'd hoped to start an import business back in Baltimore, but I won't have enough capital."

"Son, I have some money saved. I can—"

"No!" Everett immediately softened his expression. "I mean, no thank you, Father. I know you mean well, but I have to stand on my own two feet. Whatever business venture I invest in, it will be with my own assets."

His father stopped in the shade of the poplars and rubbed his gray whiskers. "I don't want to pry, son, but if you don't mind me asking, how much money was left after the estate was liquidated?"

Everett hesitated and examined his feelings. He no longer resented his father, nor blamed him for the estrangement between them for so many years. In fact, he found that he truly wanted his father's advice—a discovery that filled him with warmth.

"A little over two thousand. Certainly not the figure I thought I would inherit." He reached up and plucked a leaf from a poplar tree, twirling the stem between his thumb and forefinger.

Father slipped his hands behind his back and clasped them together. "Well, I agree with you that an import business would require more capital than two thousand." He pursed his lips and frowned, and Everett could see the thoughts turning over in his father's head. Finally, the older man spoke again.

"Willow Creek has been in need of a freighting company for quite a while. Every time I place an order for merchandise, I have to wait until one of the freighters from Dubuque or Manchester can schedule a run north. Sometimes my goods sit in their freight office for two or three weeks before they can get them here." He stared in the direction of town and rubbed his mustache with one finger. "Old Cully at the livery has complained about how long it takes to get harness parts, and Jake Peabody had to shut down the mill last year for more than two months because he was waiting for a new gear to be delivered."

His father turned a thoughtful gaze upon Everett and tipped his head. "Son, you have a business background already, so establishing such a venture shouldn't be too difficult for you."

Everett wasn't sure what running a freight operation entailed, but if his father's assessment was an indication, the town definitely had a need for the enterprise. "This is interesting, but I don't want to leap into a business about which I know nothing. Would you have time later to talk this out and help me put some plans on paper?"

Father grinned. "Of course. We can talk about it now if you like. I have the rest of the afternoon and evening."

His emotions were already dueling where Tillie was concerned, and he didn't wish to discuss his financial future in her presence. He glanced toward the house through the low-hanging branches of the poplar trees. Pearl stood on the porch, and Tillie walked away from the house in the direction of town, pausing to turn and wave back at Pearl. He and his father could discuss the business possibility in private after all, but a twinge of guilt assailed him at the thought of Tillie walking home alone. Perhaps he should have offered. . . No, he shouldn't.

three

Tillie peeked in Everett's direction from the corner of her eye but couldn't find him without turning her head. Her father, seated beside her in the pew, raised one eyebrow at her. She could almost hear his unspoken admonition and returned her attention to the man in the pulpit at the front of the room.

Pastor Witherspoon closed his Bible and made some closing comments, exhorting the worshippers to take the morning's message with them and apply it in their lives. *"Bear ye one another's burdens."* How might she go about helping Everett carry the burden of disfigurement? Her Da never seemed to be bothered by the scars *he* bore, and likewise she and her mother and siblings were so accustomed to Da's appearance, they barely took notice of the gash that trailed across his cheek and the bridge of his nose. Were Everett's scars still too fresh? Or perhaps they ran deeper than one could see on the outside.

Tillie heard the church door creak, and a slice of sunlight fell across the floorboards next to her. She risked a surreptitious glance and caught a glimpse of Everett just as he slipped out. If she waited for the preacher's closing prayer, she might miss him. She caught her bottom lip in her teeth and chafed, her feet itching to follow Everett. Finally, the pastor raised his hands for the benediction. Tillie tiptoed to the door and prayed Pastor Witherspoon's voice would cover the squeaky hinge. She stepped out and quickly scanned the churchyard. She located Everett closing the distance to the parked wagons and buggies with his long strides. The low-hanging branches of the cedars and the few white pines appeared to be his destination.

As soon as her feet hit the dirt at the bottom of the steps, she broke into a trot, but she didn't call out Everett's name until she was well away from the church.

"Everett, wait."

He slowed his forward progress and cast a brief glance over his shoulder, annoyance outlining his posture. He took a few more steps, as if he pretended not to hear her. For a moment she wondered if he would ignore her altogether. When he reached the deepest shadows of the trees, he stopped. His shoulders heaved with a great sigh.

"Everett." Tillie panted with exertion. Everett's reclusive tendencies frustrated her, but Da's repeated admonitions for compassion echoed in her memory. She stopped a few feet from where Everett stood cloaked in shadows. "I'm sorry to hold you up. I've wanted to tell you something for a while, but—" She planted one hand on her hip. "You're a hard person to nail down."

Everett turned, presenting his left side to her. It was nearly impossible to see his facial expression as he stood in the shadows and she in the bright sunlight.

"What was it you needed to tell me?" Impatience threaded his tone.

A sudden burst of unaccustomed shyness overtook her tongue, and she fidgeted with her hands. "I've pondered for months how to say this." She hooked her fingers together to stop their nervous twitching and raised her eyes to the silhouette of his profile. Her heart performed a curious flutter, and the words she wanted to say tangled in her throat. She covered her mouth and coughed.

Everett turned and cast a glance toward the church, where

the door remained closed, the congregation still inside. His chest rose and fell, as if he was trying to fend off anxiousness. She only had a moment to say what was on her mind and heart because she knew folks would come spilling out into the churchyard any moment. She drew in a breath.

"Everett, it takes an extraordinary man to put aside his own safety and demonstrate the kind of compassion you showed last year. Had it not been for your bravery and mercy, Miss Pearl and your father would surely have died in that fire. I just wanted you to know that I think you are a man of great courage and character." She glanced over her shoulder at the church, where the pastor had stepped out and stood by the door to greet the worshippers as they departed.

"Thank you," Everett mumbled. "If you'll excuse me. . ."

"Everett, wait."

He halted but a stiff sigh blew past his lips.

She took a step closer, and the patchwork of sunlight and shadows played across her eyes. "My da is an amazing man. He has such a tender, giving heart. I've never known another man who expressed his love for his family in the way he sees to their needs like Da. Your act of self-sacrifice reminds me of him."

Apparently forgetting to hide his scars, Everett widened his eyes and turned to fully face her. She waited for him to respond, but no reply was forthcoming.

Tillie dropped her gaze and stared at her clasped fingers. "Well, that's all I wanted to say. I—I guess I should let you go now."

Everett didn't seize the opportunity to escape the way he normally did. She glanced up in time to see him toss a glance at the parishioners who were gathering in the churchyard, and then he turned his attention back to Tillie.

"That's a very kind thing for you to say." He cleared his throat, and his hand trailed up to his face, even though the shadows concealed the scars he tried to hide. "I can see you are very close to your father, so for you to make such a comparison is very generous. Thank you, Tillie."

A smile unfurled from deep within her and found its way to her face. For a brief moment, she basked in the pure pleasure Everett's reply birthed in her heart. But the glow was short-lived. As quickly as Everett's guard had fallen away, he snatched it back into place. He tugged the brim of his hat down.

"Please excuse me." He turned abruptly and strode beyond the shade of the thick trees and down the boardwalk, disappearing around a corner into an alley.

Frustration niggled at her. Every time Everett raised his hand to hide his face, she longed to grasp that hand and pull it away. She wished she could make him understand his scars made no difference to her. She pondered the thought. Was that really true? Maybe his scars did make a difference, but not in the way he thought. She found his scars noble, even virtuous. They stood for something that proved the character of the man. If only she could help him see his scars the way she saw them.

Pastor Witherspoon's message about listening to God's voice and heeding His nudges to help carry the burdens of others echoed in her mind and heart. But what if God seemed to be nudging her in the direction of a stone wall?

❧

Everett looked out the dusty window of the empty building. Roland Sewell, the bank's rotund president, stood outside on the boardwalk, fanning himself with his hat and mopping his forehead with a handkerchief. Everett suspected the portly gentleman with thinning gray hair felt uncomfortable in his presence. Why else would the man elect to remain outside in the hot sun while Everett looked over the building he was considering leasing?

The location at the edge of town, directly across the street from the livery, was perfect for a freight operation. There was a good view of the main street and plenty of room for wagons to pull up and unload. Everett looked through the door that separated the larger front portion of the building from a small, private area in the rear and scrutinized the space. The back room would suffice as an office, while the front could serve as an adequate work and storage area.

Everett tugged his cravat a bit higher around his neck and stepped to the open doorway. "Mr. Sewell, the building has possibilities, but since there is no corral or other accommodation for livestock, I'll have to check with Mr. Cully at the livery to see if arrangements can be made to house the horses I'm planning on purchasing."

The man's gaze flitted over Everett. A wince of pity and revulsion flickered across his expression, neither of which Everett could abide. He turned away from the banker with the pretense of studying the framing around the door. "If the terms of the lease are still what we discussed earlier, I'd like to proceed."

"Very well, Mr. Behr. I can have the lease ready for your signature in a few days." Sewell slapped his hat back on his head and stepped off the boardwalk. "Good day."

"Good day," Everett mumbled, certain the retreating man couldn't hear him. He pushed back encroaching resentment and sighed. Roland Sewell was one person. Willow Creek was full of people who surely viewed Everett with repugnance. He might as well accept it. He pulled his hat lower to shade his face more fully and headed across the street to talk to the owner of the livery.

Poking his head in the stable door, he didn't see anyone about. "Mr. Cully?"

A thumping sound drew his attention to the rear stalls, where a grizzled, bent man stomped his feet on the packed dirt floor, apparently trying to dislodge a foreign substance from his boots.

"Mr. Cully?"

"Hold your britches on. I'm comin'." The livery owner sounded like he'd been chewing on gravel.

"Might I have a few minutes of your time, sir?"

The liveryman snorted. "Sir? Just who do you think you're talkin' to, sonny?"

"I beg your pardon, Mr. Cully."

"Ain't no need to be beggin', and my name ain't *mister*. It's just plain Cully. I don't answer to nothin' else." He dusted his grimy hands on his equally grimy pants. "A man who lives, eats, and cleans up after horses don't need no mister in front of his name." He plopped his hands on his hips. "Well? Speak your piece. I ain't got all day."

Everett cleared his throat. "I've come to discuss a business proposition, that is, if you have the time."

"Got more time than money, young fella. What's on your mind?" He clomped over to a large bin, apparently expecting Everett to follow him, and scooped grain into two wood buckets.

The dimly lit interior of the stable lent a shroud of comfortable darkness. "Well, mister. . .I mean, Cully, I'm Everett Behr, and—"

"I know who you are. You're Hubert's boy." He set the buckets down and mopped his brow.

Everett blinked in surprise. "Yes, Hubert Behr is my father." He couldn't decide if he should be put off or amused by Cully's manners, so he decided to come right to the point.

"I'm planning on renting the building across the street—"

"I seen you and old man Sewell jawin' over yonder."

It was all Everett could do to hold back a snort of laughter. Cully appeared to have quite a few years on Roland Sewell, so to hear the livery owner refer to the banker as an old man threatened to undo Everett's quiet dignity.

"Um, yes, I'll be leasing the building from Mr. Sewell for the purpose of starting a freighting operation based here in Willow Creek. I'd like to contract with you to stable my horses."

Cully's thick eyebrows sprang up into his hairline. "You don't say! That's some of the most welcome news I've heard in a while. A freightin' business, right here in Willow Creek?" Cully slapped Everett on the back. "Young fella, you bring your horses here whenever you're ready. I'll give you a fair deal."

&

Gideon Maxwell led a glossy black Belgian gelding around the yard for Everett's appraisal. "He's only four years old, but he's gentle and steady. Since he and the other three were broke to harness and trained together, they're well matched. They'll pull in pairs or in a four up."

Everett surveyed the four horses before him. "Magnificent animals. It's hard to believe a horse as big and muscular as this can be so gentle."

Gideon patted the black's neck. "That's one of the reasons I chose to breed Belgians. They're strong and have great endurance, and they also have a wonderful temperament, which makes them trustworthy with families."

The big gelding snorted and turned to look in Everett's direction, as if investigating his prospective new owner. Everett rubbed the horse's velvety nose. "I'm quite impressed. I believe these four horses will serve me well." He gave the black a pat on the neck. "What are their names?"

"I reserve the privilege of naming the horses for the buyers." Gideon grinned at him. "You get to think of four names. So when do you think you'll be ready to start your freighting operation?"

"I sent a telegram yesterday to Julien House Hardware Company in Dubuque. They've recently become a supplier of Springfield wagons." Everett stood aside while Gideon led the big gelding back to the corral. "I hope to send a man to Dubuque later this week to pick up the wagon."

"This town sure can use a freighting company. Let's go into the house and draw up the papers."

Everett pulled off his coat and hat and crossed the yard to lay them on the seat of the buggy he'd borrowed from Cully's livery. He'd been so engrossed in watching the splendid draft horses go through their paces, he'd forgotten about concealing his scars, but Gideon didn't seem to notice. As Everett followed his host to the two-story whitewashed house, Gideon's wife, Tessa, stepped out the front door with a young child on her hip. Tillie O'Dell followed on Tessa's heels. Everett instinctively ducked his head and tugged his cravat up higher around his neck till it hid his lower jawline. He glanced over his shoulder where his hat lay atop his coat on the buggy seat.

Tessa stopped on the top step of the porch. "Gideon, Tillie and I have been working on some quilt patterns together, and I was planning to take her home, but Susan is a little feverish." She brushed her hand over the child's forehead. "I'm afraid she might be coming down with something."

Before Gideon could reply, Tillie stepped forward and joined her friend on the step. "Tessa, I told you I could walk. It's only about four miles."

A feeling of tightness that had nothing to do with his

collar or cravat crept around Everett's throat. The very sound of Tillie's voice rained like soft mercy-drops on his ears. He'd never known such a feeling before, and it surely bewildered him now. The breeze caught her honey-blond hair and wisped it across her face. The curve of her cheek was interrupted by a tiny dimple that accented her smile. She might not possess the ravishing beauty of some of the socialites back east, but her gentle manner and soft smile arrested him, and her Irish green eyes held him captive.

Heat climbed Everett's neck and made the scars along his jawline sting. Sorrow pricked him. Why did God taunt him with the illusion of being attracted to a young lady like Tillie?

What a joke. It wasn't as if he was Tillie's beau. She was a mere acquaintance and could never be anything more.

"Is that all right with you, Everett?"

He startled at the sound of his name. Gideon stood looking at him with expectation and a hint of amusement.

"Um. . .I'm sorry, is what all right?"

Gideon grinned, deepening Everett's level of discomfort. "This paperwork will only take a few minutes. Would you mind driving Tillie home in your buggy?"

His gaze shot to the porch, where Tillie stood wide-eyed and blushing. Drive her home? Refusing would be rude and ungallant, but the very thought of sitting in such close proximity to her for four miles tied his tongue into knots and made it hard to breathe. A sense of motion jarred him, and he realized he'd nodded his head.

Gideon motioned him inside, and they made short work of the bill of sale for four horses. As Everett counted out the purchase price, his hands shook in anticipation of having Tillie for a traveling companion.

Outside in the yard, Gideon helped Tillie into the buggy,

and Everett breathed a sigh of relief that she'd be sitting to his left, where she couldn't view the scarred side of his face. His heart galloped as he climbed into the buggy seat beside Tillie, and he had an urgent need for a drink of water, but there was no turning back now. He released the brake and slapped the reins gently on the horse's rump.

Tillie waved at her friends as the buggy pulled away from the house. "I hope Susan feels better soon," she called to Tessa.

She turned and settled back into the seat beside him. "Thank you for the ride, Everett. I know it's out of your way, and I apologize for the inconvenience. If you like, you can just drop me off in town, and I can walk the rest of the way. It's not terribly far."

Her tone held no pretense. All the young women back in Baltimore were consumed with the obligatory society protocol. Tillie's lack of social status would have made his grandmother swoon, but as his father had pointed out on a few occasions, Willow Creek wasn't Baltimore.

He swallowed hard a few times to push down the boulder that had taken up residence in his throat and sucked in a deep breath. "Nonsense. Of course I'll drive you home."

Tillie squirmed a bit in the seat, giving him the impression of discomfort. Was she embarrassed to be seen with him? She'd made a point of speaking with him in the churchyard, but perhaps riding with him in a buggy indicated more than friendship—something she didn't want misunderstood by anyone who might see them together.

The next mile passed in awkward silence. Sweat popped out on his brow, and he ignored his proper upbringing and dragged his shirtsleeve across his face.

"Oh Everett, look." He jumped when Tillie clutched his arm and pointed. He followed the direction she indicated and noticed nothing but a few clumps of small purple flowers.

"Would you mind stopping for a minute so I can pick some of those violets? They're my favorite."

He pulled the mare to a stop and watched as Tillie hopped down and ran across the rutted road. She fell to her knees and began picking the purple blossoms and gathering them into a bouquet. As she held them to her face and closed her eyes, Everett's breath caught. What a picture she made. His heart picked up speed and thrummed double time. He stepped down and offered her a hand up when she returned to the buggy with her nosegay of violets. Was it his self-consciousness or Tillie's nearness that caused his heart to resemble Cully's hammer at the forge?

four

Everett checked another item off the bill of lading on his clipboard. A year ago, he'd never have believed he'd find enjoyment in earning a living by the sweat of his brow. Though not familiar with physical labor, he discovered it suited him. Most of the time he worked alone, content to shut himself off from the rest of the townsfolk, toiling over tally sheets, invoices, and inventories in the back office or building sturdy shelves in the front room. He'd even learned to harness the teams and hitch them to the wagon. When he fell into bed at the end of an exhausting day, he felt a satisfaction he'd never known before. The local merchants and business owners were quick to contract his services, giving him cause to wonder if he'd need to purchase a second wagon and another team by next year.

"Good morning, son."

Everett glanced up to see his father coming in his direction. He set down the clipboard he was holding and pulled a handkerchief from his pocket to wipe his perspiring forehead. "Good morning." He jerked his thumb in the direction of the crates and barrels in the back of the sturdy Springfield wagon. "Most of this load is the goods you ordered three weeks ago. As soon as I get everything inventoried and checked off the bill of lading, I'll have the fellow I hired bring them over to the mercantile."

A grin tweaked his father's mustache. "It used to take at least six weeks to get merchandise, and even then sometimes I had to send someone to take a wagon to Waterloo, Manchester, or

36

Dubuque to pick up goods from the freight depots there."

Gratification seeped into Everett's breast. Since the fire, he'd struggled to feel useful. Since he now provided the community with a needed service, perhaps he wasn't a throwback after all. He cautioned himself, however. Just because the community appreciated having a freight company in town didn't mean they could look at him without shuddering.

"Your business seems to be growing, even in the short time since you've opened your operation." His father rubbed his chin. "What's it been. . .three, four weeks?"

Everett's smile tugged on the scarred tissue along his jaw. "It's been a little over a month since I opened, and I already have enough work to keep me busy."

"You say you've hired a man?"

"Yes, only two or three days a week right now, but if business continues the way it has, I might ask him if he'd like to work every day." Everett reclaimed the clipboard and pulled his pencil from behind his ear. "You probably know him. His name is Ben Kiefer."

"Oh sure, I know Ben. He's a nice young man." His father stuck his thumbs in his belt. "What does his job entail?"

Everett counted spools of wire and checked them off the invoice on the clipboard. "Mostly he drives the runs to and from the other towns around here, since he's more familiar with the area. He helps load and unload, and he learned pretty quickly how to inventory the goods." He paused and then added, "And when he's here, he'll be handling most of the face-to-face transactions."

A slight flinch of sorrow shadowed his father's face, but thankfully he didn't argue the point. Instead he tugged his watch from his pocket and flipped open the cover. "It's time I open the mercantile door for business before folks think I've closed down and retired. I'll be waiting for Ben to bring the supplies around." He snapped the watch closed and tucked it back into his pocket, clapped Everett on the shoulder, and set off toward the center of town.

Everett checked the bill of lading once more before starting to unload the items slated to go to recipients other than the mercantile. With a grunt of effort, he dragged a crate marked FRAGILE—CHINAWARE addressed to the hotel and hoisted it off the tailgate to the boardwalk. Just as he set it down gingerly, something warm and furry brushed his arm. Startled, he released the crate and yanked his arm back, nearly falling over a skinny gray cat who regarded him with great yellow eyes.

"Watch out, you mangy cat." He scowled at the animal, who took a dignified seat with its tail curled over its front paws. "Where did you come from anyway?"

The cat continued to stare as though it expected Everett to bow in obeisance. One of the cat's ears bore a ragged edge, no doubt the result of one too many skirmishes, and its gray fur was dirty and dull.

"Go on, shoo." Everett waved his hand at the cat, who proceeded to stand and stretch, and then pad through the door of the freight depot like it owned the place. "Where do you think you're going? Come out of there." He followed the animal inside just in time to see it meander into his office and leap gracefully onto the desk. The cat settled down with its white paws tucked under its body.

"Well, just make yourself at home," Everett declared with his hands on his hips. He blew out a stiff breath. "You'd better be gone by the time I get back, because I'm going to need that desk."

The cat merely blinked in reply. Everett shook his head and returned to the wagon to finish sorting the crates. He climbed up into the wagon bed and bent to haul a crate to the edge of the tailgate when a hard object hit him sharply on his backside. He jerked upright and was met with hoots of glee. Three boys, ranging in age from around eight years to perhaps ten or eleven, pointed fingers at him and laughed uproariously.

"See? I told you he was just like a freak in a circus." The tallest boy elbowed the lad who held the slingshot. "Hey, mister, we need a scarecrow out in our cornfield. You want the job?" The trio continued to jeer, and Everett stood, stiffened with anger and embarrassment. They were only children, but their mocking filled him with humiliation. Fire rushed up his neck and into his face, searing his ears. How many people on the street heard their insulting taunts? The boy in the middle poked another stone into the slingshot and prepared to launch it in Everett's direction.

"Johnny Frasier, Billy Snipes, and William Curtis, you boys stop that this instant!"

Everett spun in the direction of the reprimanding voice. Tillie stood a few yards away, a basket over one arm and the other hand on her hip. Mortification strangled him when he realized she'd witnessed the whole thing.

Tillie took several steps toward the boys, who glanced back and forth for a way of escape. "I have a good mind to take a switch to all three of you, but I'm sure your parents can do a better job than I can." She narrowed her eyes at the trio. "Don't you know who this man is? He's a hero. He saved two people from certain death last year when the boardinghouse caught fire and was burned in the process. You all ought to be ashamed of yourselves. Now, go on home, all of you. And you'd better tell your parents what happened here today, or I will."

The boys raced off, and Tillie turned apologetic eyes on

Everett. But he was in no mood for her pity. He snatched his clipboard, jumped down off the wagon, and stalked toward the depot door.

"Everett, wait."

He didn't stop. Instead he pushed a crate aside and sought refuge in the back office. He sucked in a noisy breath through clenched teeth. The words *Just go away and mind your own business* stung the tip of his tongue, but he bit down and held them at bay. His face still flamed, and he kept his back to her.

"Everett, I'm so sorry."

"Why?"

He heard her sigh. "Those boys need to learn some manners."

He turned just enough to see Tillie standing in the doorway between the front room and his office. "They're children. They don't know any better. Some people go through their entire lives without any heed to the rudeness of their words."

He heard her soft footsteps on the wooden floor behind him. When she touched his elbow, he flinched as though she'd poked him with a sewing needle.

"I'm sure their parents will have them apologize."

He almost swung around to confront her but halted and reversed his motion, facing away from her once again. "I would rather you'd just stay out of it. I don't want them to apologize. I don't want their parents to know what happened. I just want to be left alone."

❧

Everett's terse tone nailed Tillie in her tracks. Was he implying *she* needed to learn manners? The boys' cruel taunting had stirred her ire, perhaps because for more years than she cared to count, she'd heard similar unkind remarks aimed at her own father. As a young girl, she'd retaliated in angry defense of her

Da, but she remembered his tender admonition for her to "be ye kind one to another, tenderhearted, forgiving. . . ." Learning to forgive those who said hurtful things to someone she cared about was still a struggle for her, but intentional meanness was something she couldn't abide.

She bit her lip. Judging by Everett's insistence that she stay out of it, she'd overstepped the bounds of propriety, and he'd considered her admonition of the boys rude. Vexation chafed at her, and she huffed, mentally counting to ten before her temper got the better of her. Squashing the retort that perched on her tongue, she drew in a slower, quieter breath and set her basket on the desk beside a skinny gray cat. A quick prayer for a gentle spirit winged its way heavenward, and she lowered the volume of her voice almost to a whisper.

"I apologize if I was out of line. Perhaps you're right. Since you were the one the boys insulted, I should have let you handle it. I'm sorry."

As she hoped, Everett turned halfway toward her, presenting his left side as always, and leaned closer. "I beg your pardon?"

She repeated her apology, watching Everett tip his head in her direction as she did so. Her quiet response to his sharpness produced the desired effect, as the stiffness in Everett's shoulders visibly relaxed, and he set his clipboard aside. "It's not your fault. I need to get used to things like that and learn to ignore it."

The resignation in his voice pricked her. As time went by, maybe God would show him what his scars symbolized to her. Meanwhile, all she could do was be a friend. How did one go about extending the hand of friendship to someone who continually hid himself away?

She kept her voice soft and gentle. "Everett, you are a fine, unselfish, courageous man. I pray that you can one day see that for yourself."

He gave a snort. "I see myself every day when I have to look in the mirror. Everything those boys said is true. One can hardly fault them for stating the truth."

Mild surprise raised her eyebrows, and she tilted her head to one side. "I never would have taken you for one to wallow in self-pity."

Apparently forgetting his abhorrence for letting people view his scars, he spun to face her, storm clouds gathering in his eyes. "When you're disfigured for the rest of your life, then you can pass judgment on me. Until then, I must ask you to leave now. I'm busy."

She stood her ground. "Poor Everett. He's the only person in the world who ever had to deal with difficult circumstances. It strikes me as odd, though, how a man can willingly perform such a selfless act and then feel so sorry for himself afterward. Didn't you think before you ran into that burning boardinghouse?" She lifted her gaze toward the ceiling and tapped her chin with one finger. "Hmm, perhaps entering a burning house isn't a good idea. I might be injured, or perhaps even killed. No, I think it's more prudent to let my father and Miss Pearl get out on their own."

Everett's face flooded red, and he clenched his fists. He opened his mouth but instantly clamped it shut again. Rage narrowed his eyes into slits, and his chest rose and fell as though he'd just finished a footrace. "Are you quite finished?"

She ignored the wrath that sharpened the lines of his face and dipped his eyebrows into a deep valley. Instead she extended her hands, palms turned up in entreaty. "Don't you see? That's exactly what you *didn't* do. Without any thought to your own safety and regardless of the possible consequences, you acted in pure selflessness. What you did is the noblest thing a man can do."

She lowered her hands and took a half step toward him.

Predictably, he lifted one hand to cover his scars. Her impulse was to pull that hand away, but she resisted the urge and dipped her head in a demure fashion, eyes closed and prayer winging from her heart. One day she hoped to help him forget about hiding, but that would have to wait until another day. First things first. "May I ask you a question?"

He snorted again. "Do I have a choice?"

She bit the inside of her lip to keep from smiling. "No, you don't."

The gray cat on the desk poked its inquisitive head into her basket, investigating the contents. She absently ran her fingers over its head, and the animal leaned into her touch.

"Everett, obviously the only thing on your mind when you ran into the burning house was finding your father and Miss Pearl and getting them out. You didn't think of anything else. But if you had, would you have stopped? Would you have stood out in the yard and waited for your father and Miss Pearl to come out? How would you have felt after the fire was out and you found their bodies in the burned rubble?"

Everett's shoulders rose and fell as he blew out a sigh. "That's more than one question."

This time she didn't try to conceal her smile. "I see the flames didn't completely destroy your sense of humor; they only singed it a mite." She waited for him to react to her flippant reference to his ordeal. He sent her a long, menacing glower, and she wondered if he planned to throw her out. Finally, he shook his head and looked away.

He reached out to stroke the cat, who immediately transferred its attention to Everett with a rumbling purr. A full minute went by before he answered. "I have to admit, during all those days I was lying in bed over at the doctor's house, I did think about my father and Pearl and how glad I was they were alive and safe. The pain was so intense at times, I wished I would die and be done with it. I didn't understand why God let me live. I still don't."

Grief over his statement turned her heart over. She'd never experienced anything close to what he'd been through. She started to touch his sleeve but drew her hand back, fearful that her touch might cause him to recoil. Instead she added her fingers to stroking the cat under its chin.

"You're right, I don't understand either." She tipped her head and sighed. "God brought you through the fire and let you live because it was His will. I don't think we have to understand. All He expects us to do is trust Him."

Everett jerked his head up as though her words startled him, then turned from the desk to stare out the window. His tone lost its hard edge. "Trusting is something that doesn't come easily for me. I've been learning to trust God more, but I suppose I'm not very good at it yet."

A smile, born of hope, found its way to Tillie's lips. "Just look at this dirty, half-starved creature. Why does God let it live?"

Everett turned back to look at the bedraggled cat. He shrugged and shook his head. "He just showed up this morning and acted like he owned the place."

Countless times, Tillie remembered Da instructing her or one of her siblings to perform a kind deed for someone else to take their mind off their own troubles. By focusing on another's needs, she forgot about whatever it was that caused her displeasure. Even if she couldn't understand the purpose for a hard lesson at the time, more often than not, Da's wisdom drew a lasting picture, indelibly etched in her heart. She hoped her words wouldn't anger Everett.

"Living or dying isn't up to us." She stroked the cat's ears. "God put all of us here for a purpose. Sometimes that purpose might be to save the life of another person. But such a deed can take on several forms, and we are sometimes used by God in ways we'd never expect. I think this poor cat found its way here because you need him."

A muffled sound that might have been a laugh emerged from Everett. "I think you've misplaced your good sense. Why would I need a mangy cat?"

The cat closed his eyes in obvious bliss at the attention he was receiving. She suspected Everett might catch the lesson better from God's whisper than from her lips, so she merely smiled and retrieved her basket. "I have errands to run, and I'd best get to them. Take care of that mangy cat."

five

Everett shifted in the wooden desk chair and finished adding a column of figures in the ledger. He squinched his eyes closed and rubbed the tight muscles in the back of his neck. It had been a good day, business-wise, with the addition of two more local accounts. He stepped to the window and adjusted the shade to allow the waning afternoon light to fall across his desk. He preferred keeping the shade drawn during the day, allowing only the slender shafts of sunlight that sneaked around the edges of the shade to illumine his desk. The murky shadows suited him much the way a nocturnal animal shunned the daylight.

Ben Kiefer poked his head in the office door. His straw-colored hair, dampened by perspiration, stuck out like a signpost pointing in a dozen directions. His flushed face evidenced how hard he'd been working. A faded blue chambray shirt hung loosely from his lanky frame. It came as somewhat of a surprise to Everett that he liked Ben. The young man, though a bit unpolished, might be considered a rustic bumpkin by Baltimore's society standards, but he gave Everett an honest day's work for a day's pay. And he didn't stare at Everett's scars or look away as if repulsed by them.

"Mr. Behr, I finished loading the wagon for tomorrow's run to Clermont."

"That's fine, Ben. Did you lash down the canvas? Those clouds to the west look like it might rain overnight."

Ben nodded. "Yes, sir." The young man dragged a sleeve across his face. "I'll stop by the livery on my way home and tell Cully I'll need Joshua and Jericho first thing in the morning."

The two big black geldings Ben mentioned were steady and strong, and an asset to his growing business. He recalled Ben's amusement when Everett introduced the young man to the four sturdy draft horses, all with biblical names. "You don't think you'll need the team of four?"

Ben shook his head. "No. This load isn't that heavy, and the load I'm picking up isn't a full load. Besides, I think Elijah and Solomon need an extra day of rest. If it's all right with you, I'd like to have Cully take a look at Elijah's right front shoe. I had to pry a stone out of it, and I think the shoe is a little loose."

Everett nodded his approval. "Thanks for seeing to that. Oh, wait a minute." He reached into the bottom desk drawer. "Here's your pay." He pushed an envelope across the desk. "I put a little extra in there. You drove two runs already this week, and the run tomorrow is keeping you busier than we expected. When you get back, we need to talk about you coming on full-time."

The smile on Ben's face indicated his pleasure at the unexpected bonus. "Thanks." He picked up the envelope and shoved it into his back pocket. "I plan to be on the road by daybreak." He plunked his hat in place as he headed for the door.

"Good night, Ben." Everett listened to the young man's departing footsteps across the front room followed by the opening and closing of the outside door.

The gray cat jumped from the windowsill to the desk and squeaked a meow at him as if expecting Everett to answer.

"Hello, Gray. I suppose you think it's supper time?" He rubbed the cat's head. "Sorry, but you'll have to wait a little longer. Pearl sent over a fine stew, and I promise I'll save you some." The feline produced another kittenlike chirp in response. Everett pulled his face into a grin. "You know that pitiful sound you call a meow doesn't sound very masculine. I thought male cats were supposed to yowl." He ran his hand down Gray's back and noticed he could barely feel the cat's ribs now that his new friend benefited from regular meals. Gray arched his back and leaned against Everett's stroking, a rumbling purr communicating pleasure. Everett chuckled at the cat's response to the gesture of affection. "One of these days, I'll have to try my hand at fishing the creeks around here and see if I can catch you a fresh trout. Would you like that?"

Everett scratched the cat's ears and stood, glancing out the window at the position of the sinking sun. God's paintbrush had begun to sweep the twilight sky with shades of lavender and orange edged with deeper purple. Ever since he'd established a close relationship with God, he never ceased to be amazed at the works of God's hand—things he never took the time to appreciate before.

Hunger made his stomach rumble, but when he stepped out and turned to lock the door, the nearly empty street caused him to pause and savor the freedom of not having to duck his head or tug his hat down to hide his face. Supper could wait.

He stepped off the boardwalk and crossed the street. A few people came and went from the hotel, but they paid him no attention. He strolled past the mill and admired the willows dangling their delicate tendrils along the ground near the creek bank. The breeze teased them into waving an invitation to him.

The sun hugged the horizon to his right, indicating perhaps thirty more minutes of daylight, and he intended to take advantage of the solitude. He headed toward the shadows among the willows lining the creek. A sweet calmness fell over him. Here, in the refuge offered by the sweeping willow trees and the gathering dusk, he felt no need to hide himself. He pulled in a deep breath and released it slowly. A few night birds had already begun tuning up for their evening serenade, and fireflies played tag in and out of the willows' curtains. An easy smile slipped across his face as he immersed himself in the pleasant sanctuary. A song deep within him rose to his throat, and he began humming "O for a Thousand Tongues," one of the hymns sung at last week's church service.

"The glories of my God and King. . ." "Thank You, Lord, for this place and this beauty." He gazed through the crisscrossed branches at the ever-changing colors in the sunset sky.

"Breathtaking, isn't it?"

Everett spun to see who was intruding on his seclusion. Tillie stood a few feet away, outside the willows' fringe. He instinctively took a step backward into the deepening shadows and shrugged. "Yes, it is."

"I'm sorry if I startled you." Tillie pulled her shawl around her shoulders. "I was on my way home and saw you walking this way. It's lovely this time of the evening when stillness covers the town. I love listening for the whippoorwills and watching the fireflies come out."

He couldn't blame her. The very things that had coaxed him to take an evening walk along the creek bank were the same things she mentioned enjoying.

"Yes, I love the—" He started to say *privacy*. "The quiet." He sent her a short nod and briefly touched the brim of his hat before stepping away and continuing farther down the creek bank. A flat rock offered a place to sit and enjoy the solace. To his consternation, Tillie followed and took a seat on the grass a few feet away. His initial inclination—resentment—melted before it grabbed hold of him. Instead curiosity niggled. He bent and picked up a few pebbles and tossed them into the gurgling water.

Tillie said nothing, and Everett was glad, if not surprised. He recalled the Sunday Pearl invited Tillie to dinner. Her endless chatter in the wagon on the way home that day nearly drove him to jump out and walk. At least this evening she didn't feel the need to fill every moment with conversation. She leaned forward and plucked a few clover stems, setting them into the water and watching as the gentle current wound around a few rocks and carried them downstream. He studied her out of the corner of his eye but found it unnecessary to hide his observation, since she leaned her head back and closed her eyes as she took in a deep breath. A small smile tipped the corners of her lips.

After a few minutes she glanced sideways at him, a playful look in her eye. "Would you think me scandalous and unladylike if I took off my shoes and stockings and dipped my feet in the creek?"

Everett almost chuckled out loud. "Not at all. I was just thinking of doing the same thing."

They both removed their shoes and let the cool water run over their toes. Everett couldn't remember ever doing something so undignified, even as a child. What other simple pleasures had he missed because he'd been reared by a grandmother who put more stock in social standing than enjoying the gifts God gave His children?

Tillie sighed. "Ahh, that feels so good."

Everett took in her profile, and her expression was pure bliss. Of course her feet must be tired. He presumed she didn't have much opportunity to sit down during the day, working in the hotel dining room. Less than a year ago, he'd held Tillie in disdain for her menial job. Odd, how the thought of Tillie's occupation no longer filled him with scorn. On the contrary, he felt a new respect for her, working as hard as she did. No one could accuse her of being lazy.

"Won't your family wonder where you are?" Everett almost bit his tongue the moment the inquiry slipped out. He didn't mean for it to sound as though he was anxious for her to leave. But she didn't seem to take offense.

"No. Sometimes when I work the supper shift, I don't get home until after dark." She flicked a mosquito from her arm. "When I have to work late, my brother and sister do some of my chores."

Everett raised his eyebrows. On top of working at the hotel, she had household chores to perform. "Doesn't your brother work at the mercantile for my father?"

She splashed her foot in the creek. "My brother Phillip. Regan and Grady help with my chores when I get home late. Grady's only ten, but he likes to think he can do the work of a grown-up."

"And who is Regan?"

Tillie placed her hands on the grass behind her and leaned back. "My oldest sister. Well, I mean, I'm the oldest, and Phillip is the next oldest at fifteen, but Regan is the sister closest to me in age at fourteen. Then comes Fiona—she's twelve. Then Grady. Brenna is my youngest sister—she's six. And the baby is Cory—he's four."

"Such a large family," Everett mused. "It must be noisy at mealtimes. I never had any siblings."

Tillie's laugh blended with the sound the water made as it danced over the rocks. Together the harmony played on Everett's ear like a gentle interlude.

"The only time it's not noisy around our house is when Da reads the Bible and prays with all of us before bedtime. Even Cory has learned to be quiet and listen." She grinned. "But you're right. Such blarney around the breakfast table every morning. And supper time. *Whist!* What a chatter. Da claims he can't even hear himself ask for seconds."

Everett tipped his head back and laughed. "All of a sudden I feel my meals are very lonely. It's just me and the cat."

Tillie shifted around and began drying her feet on the grass. "So you decided to keep that mangy cat, did you?"

"He's not so mangy anymore." Everett followed Tillie's example and twisted around to set his dripping feet on the rock beside him. "He's getting sleek and fat. I think he's adopted me."

Her musical laughter gifted his ears once more. "Have you given this fat cat a name?"

"Gray."

"Gray what?"

"The cat's name. I just started calling him Gray. He doesn't seem to care. He doesn't come when I call him anyway, unless I have food in my hands."

Tillie's hands halted in their task of pulling on her shoes. "Gray? What an unimaginative name. I think I would have named him. . .Sir Lancelot or Solomon."

"That's the name of one of my horses."

"You named your horse Sir Lancelot, but you named the cat Gray?"

"No, Solomon. I bought four horses from Gideon Maxwell, and I gave them all biblical names."

Tillie cocked her head to one side as if weighing his choice of names for his livestock as he described each animal. They continued for a few more minutes, laughing as he relayed an amusing story of Gray bringing a mouse to him, only the mouse was still alive. Tillie responded with an account of one of her brothers sneaking a squirrel into the house that he intended to keep as a pet until it got loose from its box and led the entire family on a merry chase. Everett couldn't remember a time when he'd laughed so much, or enjoyed a conversation with such a lovely young woman.

Realization hit Everett that they'd spent a half hour in each other's company and he felt completely at ease, unlike the Sunday afternoon he'd worked so hard to distance himself from her. The gathering darkness surely had something to do with it, but at some point he became aware that while she looked him directly in the eye, she hadn't once stared at him. He detected neither pity nor repulsion in her expression or tone. Being in Tillie's company as dusk settled in around them was more pleasant that he could have imagined.

She finished tying her shoes and tugged the hem of her skirt down to cover her shoelaces as she stood. The murmuring water provided background music. Shadows blended with the encroaching night, and Everett rose and faced her fully.

Tillie bent to retrieve her reticule. "Do you go walking in the evening often?"

"Not really, but it is quite pleasant this time of day, isn't it?" A flicker of hope tickled his stomach.

She dipped her head, and in the retreating streaks of the sunset, Everett saw a demure smile grace her lips. "Perhaps. . . I might see you again out walking some evening."

The pinpoint of hope became a glimmer. "Perhaps." In unison they stepped away from the grassy creek bank and walked toward the edge of town, Everett measuring his strides to match hers.

Their easy conversation continued, and before he realized what was happening, he'd walked with her nearly all the way to her family's farm a mile past town. He hadn't intended to walk her home, but the relaxed manner Everett discovered in the twilight made being with her so pleasant that his self-consciousness faded like the daylight. To his surprise, they now stood at the edge of her father's cornfield. The small farmhouse, silhouetted against the darkening sky, didn't look large enough to hold the number of family members Tillie had told him about, but the welcoming lamplight that spilled from its windows opened its arms in a warm greeting. He wondered what it might be like to step through the door of one's home and embrace loved ones. A momentary picture flitted through his mind. What if Tillie were the one greeting him at the door with her gentle ways and ready smile? The image stole quietly into his mind and lingered.

"I'd best go in now. Da and Ma will be wondering about me."

Tillie's soft voice jolted him out of his reverie. "Oh—uh, yes, of course. Well, good night, Tillie." His hands seemed to not have an occupation, for they fidgeted between clasping together and seeking refuge in his pockets.

"Thank you for walking me home, Everett. It was very kind of you."

He couldn't be sure in the darkness, but her voice sounded like she was smiling.

❧

All the way home, Everett chided himself for his foolish thoughts. Tillie was merely being polite and charitable. She might concede to sit with him in the shadow of the willows or walk with him at nightfall when nobody could see them, or even speak to him in the churchyard after hearing a sermon on compassion. But no respectable young woman would care to be seen in public with the likes of him. The garish light of day would always reveal the ugliness he would never be able to hide.

He clenched his fist and punched the side of his leg as he strode toward town. "I suppose, Lord, that I should get used to the idea that I'll live out the rest of my days alone." He shook his head. "I accept the blame, Lord. The way I tried to separate my father and Pearl last year, the arrogance that drove me to be so hateful and manipulating—Lord, I know I have no right to think I could find happiness with anyone. You've forgiven me, and I'm grateful. I just have to learn to live with. . .with a face that offends people."

He slowed his steps as he passed the grove of cedars that edged the churchyard. Their pungent scent wafted on the night air. "I know I shouldn't allow myself to think about how things might be with Tillie. Because they can never be." He crossed the street to the mercantile, cut through the alley, and climbed the stairs at the back of the building.

Gray greeted him, having found his way between the freight depot and Everett's living quarters over the mercantile. Everett absently rubbed the cat's head. Gray didn't mind his scars. Neither did God. He might never experience the intimate communion a husband and wife shared, but God's all-consuming love would be enough. After all, God saved him from the fire. Surely there must be something more God intended for him other than running a freight company.

"God, it isn't that I doubt Your sovereignty. I just can't imagine how You can use somebody like me—somebody who looks like me." He crossed the room and opened the window, pushing the curtain aside and taking a lungful of scented night air. The tree frogs and cicadas were in full voice, and the whippoorwills answered in harmony. It seemed every creature had a purpose—everyone but him.

six

Familiar chatter greeted Tillie like a welcoming hug the moment she opened the front door. Her sisters Regan and Fiona giggled while Phillip teased Grady about the frog the lad had carried home in his pocket. Ma sat in the rocker brushing Brenna's hair, admonishing Grady to take the frog outside and threatening to take a switch to Phillip if he didn't stop his endless teasing. Little Cory clamored for his share of attention while Da leaned back in his threadbare, overstuffed chair by the fireplace.

"Ah, and here's our lovely Matilda, come to join the family chorus of all this heavenly music." Da sent her a lopsided grin.

"Pfft! Music, he says." Ma waved the hairbrush, gesturing to her noisy offspring. "The song of the angels in heaven surely must fall on the ears sweeter than this commotion." She set the brush aside and nudged Brenna toward the ladder that led to the loft. "Off with you now. Go and put on your nightdress. Scoot." She rose and pointed to Grady. "Take your little brother and help him wash his face and put on his nightshirt. Girls, stop that giggling, and finish up the dishes. Phillip, did you fill the wood box?"

Phillip traded playful punches with Grady. "Yes'm."

Tillie smiled at what Da deemed heavenly music and gave her mother a peck on the cheek. "Glad I wasn't too late to take part in the concert."

"Humph. The hen has ruffled feathers until her flock is grown." Ma slid a sideways look in her direction. "I wish you didn't have to work so late. You know I don't like you walking home alone in the dark." Without waiting for a reply, her mother shooed young Cory up the ladder to comply with her instructions and hurried Regan and Fiona through their task.

Tillie fetched the plate Ma always left in the warming oven for her and sniffed appreciatively at the rabbit stew. "I wasn't alone. Everett Behr walked me home."

The confusion of herding the youngsters to prepare for bed seemed to occupy her mother's attention, but a swift glance at Da told her that he might have a few questions later about her escort. Her father's deep green eyes fastened a silent inquiry on her as she ate her supper. A measure of comfort made her heart smile. Da's protective watch-care over his brood was a sweet assurance she'd treasured from childhood.

The younger siblings, clad in nightclothes, descended the loft ladder and assembled on the floor around Da's chair, tumbling over each other like tussling puppies. He opened the worn pages of the Bible and hooked his wire spectacles over his ears. Once the round lenses perched on his nose, he cleared his throat and began to read, capturing each child's attention. Even little Cory, snuggled on Ma's lap, hushed while Da read. Tillie memorized the picture, hoping to re-create the scene for herself one day.

Scriptures read and prayers said, Ma hustled the young ones up to the loft to tuck them in and distribute good-night kisses. Tillie slipped over and sat on the floor in front of her father, smiling at his upraised eyebrows. "What is it you want to know, Da?"

He blew out a breath through pursed lips. "Well now, girl, how is it you think I'm wantin' to know somethin'?"

She couldn't stop the smile from spreading across her face. "You're wondering about Everett walking me home."

Da lifted one shoulder in a noncommittal shrug, but the twinkle in his eyes gave him away. "I might be wonderin' just a wee bit." He cocked his head toward her and peered over the top of his spectacles. "Don't mean to be stirrin' the pot here, but is this the same Everett Behr who looked down his nose at you last year when he found out you worked in the hotel dinin' room?"

Tillie watched the flames lick the logs in the fireplace, considering her answer. "No, Da, he's not the same. I believe God has used the events of the past several months to change him. He has a humility he didn't have before. But more than that, he reminds me of someone I admire and respect more than anyone on this earth."

Da removed his spectacles and tucked them into his shirt pocket. "Respect isn't somethin' you want to give away freely, daughter. It has to be earned. You'd best be makin' sure o' that."

Pride swelled in her chest. "Da, the person I admire and respect the most in this world is you. The way you love your family and work hard, your integrity and faith, are the things I love most about you. I hope to one day marry a man just like you."

A tiny frown pinched Da's brows as he looked away and sniffed. Raising his arm, he blotted his face on his sleeve before returning his gaze to his eldest. "Girl, you've kissed the blarney stone for certain." He leaned close and whispered, "But sure and you know how to get to your old da's heart." He patted her hand. "So you're sweet on this fellow, are you now?"

Tillie wrapped her arms around her knees and released a soft sigh. "I'm not quite sure yet if I'd call it that. When he first came to town last year, he was so handsome—I was just as smitten as every other girl in town. But now. . ."

"Now?" Da left the obvious unspoken. Everett was no

longer handsome, at least in the eyes of some people.

She brushed a wisp of hair from her face. "I'm drawn for a different reason. A man who puts aside his own well-being and faces danger to save the lives of two people is a man with a depth of character that sets him apart. Handsomeness doesn't seem so important anymore." She paused, more to consider her own words than her father's reaction. "It's what's inside that makes a man, and I want to get to know the man Everett Behr. I want to learn what kind of character moves a man to suffer what he did on behalf of someone else."

She raised her eyes to the ceiling and listened to the soft murmur of good nights being exchanged overhead in the loft. "This evening as I was leaving work, I saw him walking alone. He always ducks his head, or turns away, or lifts his hand to cover his face when people are near. But as the sun set and the darkness came on, it seemed he didn't feel the need to hide."

Her father nodded. "I understand a wee bit about wantin' to hide from the world."

Gratified by her father's insight, she went on. "I walked over and spoke to him, and it was as if he felt free to carry on a conversation, like the sun dropping below the horizon rendered him safe." She shook her head slightly. "I wish he understood that his scars don't matter to me."

Da absently ran one finger along the jagged scar across his face. "You grew up lookin' at my scar, daughter, so it's normal for you. It's not for Everett." He rubbed his chin. "You know that story in Jeremiah where the prophet goes to the potter's house and watches a clay pot bein' formed on the wheel? There was somethin' amiss in the clay, and the pot couldn't be useful the way it was. So the potter made it over again. That's what happened to me. I had somethin' amiss in my life, and I broke. God had to reshape me. The scar is just a reminder that I never want to go back to that place o' sin again. I'm thinkin' maybe God has made Everett over again as well." He reached out and cupped Tillie's chin, his thumb caressing her cheek. "But give him time to settle into the new vessel God's creatin' of him.

"I'm thinkin', too, that Everett wasn't the only one refined by the fire. Seems I've seen a bit of a change in you, too, my darlin'. 'Tis difficult to put a wise head on young shoulders, but I'm noticin' you've learned a deeper level o' compassion. Instead of shuttin' out the person who hurt you in the past, you've opened your heart, lettin' God show His love and carin' through you. It's proud I am of you, girl."

Tillie felt a blush rise at her father's praise. "Everett said he liked walking in the evening, and when I mentioned maybe we'd see each other again out walking, he seemed pleased." She leaned forward and looked fully into her father's face. "Da, if it's all right with you, I'd like to walk with Everett again some evening after work. He was so relaxed as we talked tonight, and I think it was because he didn't feel like he had to hide his face."

Da frowned, and at first Tillie thought he was going to forbid her to see Everett under the cloak of darkness. His eyes searched her face, and finally he laid his hand on her head. "Appearances are important, child. You must mind yourself that you don't allow people to draw the wrong conclusion." He studied her for a full minute before continuing. "I'm trustin' the way I raised you, daughter. You've heard me say such before, and there's no sense in boilin' the cabbage twice. You use good sense, and guard your reputation." A tiny smile tweaked his lips. "And whilst you're at it, guard your heart as well. Your da doesn't want to see you get hurt again." He leaned forward and placed a kiss on her forehead.

❧

Everett gave Gray a few strokes and a scratch behind the ear when the cat rubbed against his leg. "I know, old man— it's almost time to close up and go home." He glanced out the window of his office. The sun hung low in the western sky, almost touching the horizon. Perhaps another half hour until the shadows stretched into wide, sweeping cloaks. Anticipation tickled his stomach, and he purposefully disciplined his mind, returning his attention to the invoices on his desk. He flipped through a few of the papers and realized he had no idea what he'd just read.

Don't be ridiculous! Just because he happened to run into Tillie three times last week and twice already this week didn't mean she'd be waiting for him at the creek this evening. Each time they'd strolled among the thickening shadows, their conversation flowed more freely. Talking to Tillie felt. . . right. Was it so wrong to look forward to being with her, talking with her? Was he foolish for harboring memories of each evening they'd walked together, like a schoolboy carving initials into a tree trunk?

He recalled the sound of her laughter, and he pushed away from the desk. Leaning back with his hands tucked behind his head, he closed his eyes and gave himself permission to dream. A smile twitched his lips as memories of his evening walks with Tillie traced soft images across his mind. He'd had friends in Baltimore, and he'd seen a few young ladies socially. But he couldn't remember ever having a friend like Tillie. He had to admit she was more than just a friend. Sunset strolls with her at the end of the day eased his anxiety and melted away the apprehension he normally experienced with others. Tillie demonstrated no insincerity or charade, nor did she present any expectations. She encouraged him to speak his mind or sit by the creek in silence, to contemplate the intricacies of a clover blossom or count fireflies, to discuss last Sunday's sermon or regale her with Gray's hunting exploits.

The tiresome events among Baltimore's society had demanded he always present himself with proper poise and dignity. Twilight conversation with Tillie often found them dangling bare feet in the creek. Why, just a few evenings ago, they'd sat at the water's edge pitching pebbles into the current and singing "Rock of Ages," laughing as they improvised the harmony. Wouldn't the debutantes in Baltimore titter behind their hands at such a sight?

For all the pleasantness of being in her company, however, there remained the hard truth. Tillie might be a wonderful friend, but that was all she could ever be. If he were to be honest with himself, he'd have to acknowledge that he wished he and Tillie could be more. Much more. A lonely ache defined a desire for a deeper bond, but even as the idea flitted through his mind, he knew such closeness could never be realized.

He shook his head and pulled himself up to the desk. Pursuing a romantic relationship would only result in heartache for him and embarrassment for Tillie. It was her kindheartedness and generous nature that induced her to offer friendship. To expect anything more was selfish, and he'd not put her in the awkward position of having to refuse his request for courtship.

Another glance out the window told him the sun was almost gone. Gray followed Everett out the door of the depot but seemed to understand the honor of his presence was not requested as a chaperone. The feline sat and groomed himself on the boardwalk as Everett locked the door.

"I'll see you later at home." He bent to rub Gray's head and headed off toward the creek, lending his voice to a hymn sung at last Sunday's service.

"Be Thou my vision, O Lord of my heart, naught be all else to me, save that Thou art." Not remembering the rest of the words, he continued humming as he strode along. When he turned the corner at the mill, the creek came into view. The breeze swayed the willow branches, allowing him a glimpse of Tillie's blond hair catching the ebbing sunlight.

The hymn remained on his lips as he approached. He knew the moment she heard him humming, for she turned her head toward him and joined her pure soprano voice with his.

"Waking or sleeping, Thy presence my light."

He stepped over to where she sat beside the creek. She'd already shed her shoes, and her toes played in the water. Out of habit, he took a position to her right, keeping his left profile toward her.

"That's one my Da's favorites. It's an Irish hymn from the eighth century." She twirled a buttercup between her thumb and forefinger. "It's a lovely evening for hymn-singing."

"Yes, it is." He removed his shoes and let his feet dangle in the creek. "But I'm quite sure any attempt on my part to sing harmony would be an affront to the composer," he added with a chuckle. "I'm afraid I scared off all the fireflies the other night when I tried to sing with you."

Her soft giggle rained like dewdrops. "My Da can stampede cattle, but that doesn't stop him from singing. Haven't you ever seen him walking down the boardwalk in town singing?"

He'd seen her parents at church, but only the backs of their heads or from a distance across the yard. He noted she had the same color hair as her father and wondered from which parent she inherited her clear green eyes. Her question prompted a recollection. Less than a week ago he saw a man, a farmer judging by his dress, entering the mercantile singing at the top of his lungs, drawing amused looks from the townsfolk. While he didn't think it too strange for the man to be singing, he was astounded that the fellow didn't mind drawing attention to himself. Even from several paces away, the jagged scar that stretched from the man's cheekbone to the bridge of his nose was clearly visible.

"I think I may have seen him." Everett rubbed his chin. "Green bandana and singing an Irish folk song?"

Tillie laughed again and nodded. "That'd be Da."

The shadows played around them, and their growing friendship coaxed him into asking a question of a more personal nature. "What happened, Tillie?" He almost snatched the inquiry back and apologized, but Tillie's eyes held no defensiveness. "What happened to your father to leave him with such an ugly scar?"

She tilted her head to one side, a tiny, sad smile tugging at her mouth. "Da used to frequent the saloons—before he became a child of God. Sometimes he'd drink so much he couldn't find his way home."

Everett heard the wistfulness in her voice. She leaned forward and dipped her fingers in the clear running water. The obviously painful memory cut a furrow into her brow, and he started to tell her she didn't need to say any more, but she spoke again.

"I remember Ma crying in the night when Da didn't come home. I was about Brenna's age when Da got into a barroom fight. One of the men he was fighting slashed Da across the face, chest, and arm with a broken whiskey bottle." Her voice caught and softened into a hush. "He was hurt very badly. By the time a few of his friends carried him to the doctor, he'd lost a lot of blood. The doctor couldn't say for sure if he would live." Everett couldn't imagine how frightening it must have been for her as a little girl to see her father so terribly injured.

"After a while he began to heal, and Ma talked him into going to church with us. There was a visiting preacher, and for the first time in his life, Da *listened*. He decided he never wanted to cause his family so much grief again, and he asked God to forgive him and make him into a new man."

In the cloak of shadows, he heard her sigh—a soft sound full of reflection. "Da gave his heart and his life to God that day, and he says every morning when he looks in the mirror and sees the scars, he remembers how far God has brought him."

She sat back and turned to face him. "You know, it's never occurred to me to think of Da's scars as ugly. To me, they're beautiful, because they represent that precious time when God gave me back my Da."

seven

Everett polished off his wedge of apple pie and wiped his mouth on his napkin. "Delicious, Pearl. But I feel guilty for accepting so many invitations to dinner when I haven't extended any." He grinned. "Not that you'd want to eat my cooking."

Father laughed out loud. "Pearl cooked for a crowd at the boardinghouse for so many years that she's had a hard time learning how to cook just for the two of us. If you didn't come to dinner and take some of this food home with you, we'd be eating it for a week."

Pearl flapped a hand at her husband. "He's right. One of these days I'll figure out how to make a casserole that feeds two instead of twelve." She rose and began clearing the dishes. "You two go on in the living room. I'll bring the coffee in later."

Everett pushed away from the table and headed for the large leather chairs in front of the fireplace. The delectable meal and pleasant conversation made for a relaxing end to the day, but his mind wandered to the shadowy creek bank and Tillie's special company. He wondered if Tillie had walked by the creek this evening on her way home. It wasn't as if they made plans to meet. He'd never actually asked her to join him for a walk. They always left it to chance.

His father sat opposite him. "I noticed you've been seeing Tillie O'Dell."

Everett jerked his head up. How did Father know about that? Could he read his son's mind?

The twinkle in Hubert's gray eyes indicated approval. "I've seen the two of you walking together a few times as I'm closing up the mercantile. Most recently, I saw you one evening last week. I had a late delivery to make. On my way back, I went by Pastor Witherspoon's house. While he and I sat on his front porch, we saw you and Tillie off in the distance, down by the creek." He rubbed his mustache and smiled. "Tillie is a very nice young lady. I'm happy you two are getting to know each other."

Not wishing his father or Pearl to misunderstand, he cleared his throat and shook his head. "Tillie *is* a nice girl, but she's just being kind. She's nothing more than a friend." He gave a dismissive shrug and hoped his father would change the subject.

Father's bushy eyebrows came together. "Why couldn't she be more than a friend? You won't find a sweeter girl in the whole county." He uncrossed his legs and leaned forward. "Son, if you intend to pursue her, you'd best make your intentions known. I've seen how the other young fellows buzz around her. It won't be long and one of them will be asking her father for courting privileges."

A knot formed and twisted in Everett's stomach at the idea of another man courting Tillie. He'd tried having a stern conversation with his heart, pointing out the obvious disadvantages of continuing to meet Tillie for their evening strolls. It simply wouldn't do for him to lose his heart to her, especially when reciprocation was impossible. Certainly Tillie's whole purpose in forming a friendship with him was purely charitable. There was no sense in envisioning anything more. He slammed his mind's door on the scenario.

"If Tillie wants to see other fellows, that's entirely up to her. I certainly have no claim on her." He brushed an imaginary piece of lint from his cuff. When he glanced up again, the elder Behr was studying him with an unreadable expression. Everett continued, anxious not to give the wrong impression.

"Father, Tillie has been very kind to go walking with me, and I suspect she is doing so as a demonstration of compassion and mercy like Pastor Witherspoon talks about on Sundays." He absently ran his fingertips over the ridges and valleys of the mottled skin along his right jawline. "Tillie should see other fellows. I'm grateful for her benevolence, but I must find some way to tell her that she needs to accept the attention of some of these other gentlemen." He tucked his chin and frowned. "They *are* gentlemen, aren't they?"

A quiet smile spread across Father's face, stretching his salt-and-pepper beard. "Timothy O'Dell wouldn't allow anything less." He took his whiskers between his thumb and forefinger and tugged absently. "That young fellow who works for you—"

"Ben Kiefer?"

"Mm." His father's gaze wandered toward the window. "I've noticed him waiting on Sunday mornings out in the churchyard. When the O'Dells' wagon pulls up, he is usually the first one to step over and help Tillie down from the wagon."

The knot that took up residence in Everett's stomach earlier rolled over, and he clamped his teeth together. By arriving to church late every week, he didn't get to see who Tillie's admirers were. For some reason he couldn't explain, it bothered him to know Ben Kiefer was among them.

"How do you feel about that?"

Everett shook himself and focused his attention back on his father. "About what?"

Hubert smiled again. "Son, I've seen you and Tillie out walking several times. Why would you go for evening strolls together if you didn't have some feelings for her? Knowing other young men are coming around and paying attention to her must generate something inside you."

There was no point in trying to fool his father. Everett sucked in a breath and let it out slowly. "Father, you must understand that I'm not in the position to make any offers to Tillie." He slid his gaze to the window and swallowed. "All we do is go for walks in the evening when there's nobody around to see us together."

"I've seen you together." Father leaned back in his chair. "So has Pastor Witherspoon and his wife. It's not like you're hiding. You walk in plain sight of the town."

Everett dipped his head. Did he have to spell it out? A sigh stretched from his heart to his lips just as Pearl entered the living room with the coffee tray. "In the evening, it's growing dark enough so most people can't see who she's walking with. I won't embarrass Tillie by asking her. . .to accompany me in broad daylight, or allow me to escort her someplace where people will stare at the two of us. She's probably too kindhearted to turn me down, but I won't put her in that position."

Pearl set the tray down on the low table between Everett and his father. She flicked a glance in Everett's direction and poured a cup of coffee, setting it in front of him. "Everett, that's nonsense. You have so many fine qualities—I can't list them all. Any girl would consider herself lucky for such a beau." She poured two more cups of coffee and slid one toward her husband before glancing back at Everett. "I know you aren't my son, but over the past year I've grown to love you. If I could choose the best young lady this side of the Mississippi for you, I couldn't find one sweeter than Tillie."

He stirred a spoonful of sugar into his coffee and took a tentative sip of the steaming brew. "I appreciate your concern, both of you. Believe me, you don't have to tell me about

Tillie's sweetness." He wished he could dismiss it from his mind. He caught Pearl from the corner of his eye giving Father a tiny shake of her head. Her message was clear. *Leave him alone—don't push.* Everett released a relieved sigh.

Pearl lit the oil lamp on the mantel. Everett eyed the glow inside the glass globe, and his heart seized the way it always did when he looked at a flame. He pulled his gaze away and concentrated on the mug in his hands. They sipped their coffee in silence, listening to the cicadas and tree frogs singing their shrill chorus, interrupted occasionally by the call of a whippoorwill—a concert he wished he was enjoying in Tillie's company.

Everett finally set his empty cup on the tray and rose. "It's time for me to go. Gray gets crabby if he has to wait for his supper."

Pearl bustled to the kitchen and returned with a basket covered with a blue checked napkin. "I put the rest of the apple pie in here along with the chicken casserole. Now don't give it all to the cat." She patted his hand. "You remember what I said, all right?"

A tiny smile tilted his lips. "I will, and thank you. Good night, Father, Pearl."

The walk home stretched just long enough for him to do some thinking. Perhaps he should reassess this friendship with Tillie. A closer relationship could only end painfully, since it would hold no future for either of them.

"I need to put a little distance between us. Maybe I should encourage her to see other men before this goes too far." He cut down the alley and climbed the stairs to his apartment.

Gray sat patiently waiting on the landing and welcomed Everett with a squeaky meow. The cat wound himself around Everett's ankles, waiting for him to scoop out a cat-sized portion of Pearl's chicken casserole on a small plate.

As Gray enjoyed his supper, Everett recalled his father's comment about Ben Kiefer. He swallowed back the knot in his throat and ignored the tightening in his chest. Ben was a good employee and a hard worker, and Everett liked him. At least up until now.

"Don't be ridiculous." He pushed the budding resentment aside. "Ben's interest in Tillie doesn't change the kind of employee he is." He plopped down in a chair and pulled off his boots. "So what if Ben is interested in her. He's a nice guy, and she's a nice girl." Unease pierced its way into his gut.

Gray looked up from his supper plate and licked his whiskers, showing minimal interest in Everett's solo conversation.

"I suppose you think I'm being foolish."

The cat blinked and returned to his food.

"Humph. Big help you are." He lit the lamp in the sitting room and opened a book, but try as he might to concentrate, thoughts of Tillie continued to spiral in his mind.

❧

Tillie pulled her shawl up around her shoulders and sent Everett a shy smile. "It's getting a little too cool for dipping our toes in the creek. And it's beginning to get dark earlier as well." The sun had already disappeared, and the lingering light was fading fast.

A mild scowl interrupted Everett's features. For all the pleasant conversations they'd enjoyed during the summer evenings, now that August was coming to a close, he'd been mighty quiet. She'd had to remind herself not to chatter like a magpie. But if he didn't talk to her, how could she know what he was brooding about?

"How are things going with your business?"

Everett shuffled the toe of his boot in the dirt. "Good."

"Da said he ordered a new blade for the plow and it got here in only two weeks."

Everett didn't look at her but kept his gaze fixed on the worn path that traced the meandering creek. "Good."

"Mr. Kyle, the owner of the hotel, was delighted that the new fixtures he ordered for the dining room arrived so quickly."

"Hmm."

Tillie raised her eyebrows and cocked her head to one side. "And wasn't it fun watching the circus elephants parade down the middle of the street this morning?"

"Mm-hmm."

She halted in her tracks and shook her head. "Everett Behr, have you heard a word I've said?"

He jerked his head up with a look of surprise. "I beg your pardon?"

Exasperation nipped at her. Since early summer they'd shared all sorts of things with each other. But lately Everett had reverted back to the sullen moodiness he'd displayed a few months ago. What had happened to make him so aloof and preoccupied? Had she said something to offend him?

"Is something wrong?"

That tiny frown pinched Everett's brows again, and his hand slid up to cover the right side of his face. "Nothing important."

As much as she wished to prod an answer out of him, she held her tongue and pursed her lips. His distraction likely had to do with business, and she wouldn't intrude. She expelled a soft sigh as she fell back into step with him. Perhaps a change of subject might coax a smile into his eyes.

"The harvest picnic and barn dance are coming up next month, as soon as everyone has their crops in. Miss Pearl and Mrs. Witherspoon have been planning it. They've asked Dan and Sarah Miller if we can use their barn for the dance. It's scheduled for Saturday, the twenty-sixth of September."

Everett gave a soft grunt. "I heard. Ben mentioned it the other day."

"I love autumn." She schooled her voice to sound carefree. It had been a long time since she'd had to work so hard at a conversation between them. "It's a little sad to see summer go, but I love the cooler temperatures and watching the trees turn color. The harvest picnic is Willow Creek's way of saying farewell to summer and welcoming autumn."

She hesitated, hoping that bringing up the topic might plant the idea in his head, and maybe—just maybe—he'd get up the nerve to ask to escort her to the picnic and dance.

To her disappointment, he steered the conversation in another direction. "You know, Ben Kiefer's a very nice fellow. I was noticing a few days ago what a good job he's been doing. He's very diligent. I never have to tell him to do anything twice. And he's well mannered, too. And generous. You know I saw him helping that older lady—Mrs. Wagner, I think is her name. Ben carried a crate of supplies to her buggy the other day. Yes, Ben is a fine fellow."

Tillie slowed her steps and slid a sideways look at him. What did the change of seasons have to do with Ben Kiefer? "Yes," she said slowly. "I agree. Ben is a nice fellow and certainly not lazy." Was Everett trying to make a point, showering his employee with accolades?

"Yes, Ben was telling me all about that picnic and how he's looking forward to it. He said he loves the barn dances, especially if he has a good partner." His tone seemed artificially cheerful. "I sure hope he isn't disappointed."

Tillie drove her eyebrows downward into a V. "At the risk of seeming a bit foolish, what exactly is your meaning?"

He gave a noncommittal shrug. "Nothing, except that Ben Kiefer has been paying attention to you, and maybe..."

Her feet came to a halt so quickly she almost stumbled.

Planting her hands on her hips, she challenged him to finish his sentence. "Maybe, what?"

He stopped and pulled a few yellowing leaves from the dangling willows. "Maybe you should. . .pay attention back, is all I'm saying."

"Everett Behr, are you trying to aggravate me?"

He turned toward her but stopped halfway so all she could see in the shadows was his profile. "No, of course not. I'm merely suggesting that Ben might be a good candidate for an escort. That is, if you planned to attend the picnic and barn dance."

Most of the time Tillie felt proud of her Irish heritage. Other times, like now, having Irish blood coursing through her veins could be a pure trial. She sucked in a deep breath and mutely counted to ten, hoping it might tamp down her temper.

"And when exactly did God put you in charge of selecting my escort to the picnic and barn dance?"

She heard him whoosh out a breath with what sounded like frustration. He took a step closer and turned to face her fully. His eyes met hers for only a moment before he lowered his head and raised his hand up to his face. In that brief heartbeat, she read something—something forbidden to her for months because he wouldn't look straight at her. But for one instant she caught a glimpse of the agony of loneliness. When he spoke again, belligerence colored his voice.

"I'm not implying any such thing, and why are you being so stubborn?"

She bit her lip and swallowed back the retort that rose up in her throat. His purpose for pushing her in Ben's direction wasn't lost on her. That fleeting blink of insight painted the real picture of Everett's turmoil, and a keen ache skewered her heart as she realized his intention. He viewed his scars as a stone wall too high to climb and too wide to circumvent, the result of which was permanent isolation. Well, she disagreed. The question now was how to get Everett to see things from her perspective. A shouting match didn't seem prudent. Da always said the best way to avoid an argument was to refuse to argue and lower your voice. She removed her hands from her hips and adopted a more sedate posture, hoping to disarm him.

Instead of giving Everett the chance to turn away as he normally did, she turned and ran her hand through the dangling willow branches. She pulled three of them toward her and began twisting them into a braid like she did with Brenna's flaxen hair. The activity served its purpose. The fire of aggravation that had kindled a minute ago fizzled.

Only then did she trust herself to open her mouth and speak gentleness to Everett's heart. "I'm not trying to be stubborn." She continued braiding and listened for his response. A defused sigh reached her ears, and she was grateful for the darkness so Everett couldn't see her smile.

She released the willow withes and watched them untangle. "I agree with you that Ben is a fine fellow. But it would be difficult to attend the picnic and dance with him."

This time when Everett spoke, all she could hear was resignation. "I don't see what you're waiting for."

She looked at him over her shoulder. "He hasn't asked me." She returned her attention to the mangled willow curtain. "And a certain fellow I'd like to go with hasn't asked me either."

eight

Everett took the last sip of his cooling tea and rose to set his cup in the dry sink. Gray looked up at him expectantly and produced a squeaky meow.

"You've already had your supper," Everett said, holding the door open. "Go catch a mouse."

Gray ambled out, brushing Everett's leg as he passed. Everett stood in the open doorway for a few minutes, gazing at the stars flung across the inky sky. What was the verse that Pastor Witherspoon had used the previous Sunday? Everett scrunched his eyes shut in his effort to recall the scripture. It was somewhere in Isaiah—chapter 40, he thought. He closed the door and went to take up his Bible and see if he could find the words the preacher had used. Pulling up a chair, he leaned closer to the lamplight and leafed through the pages. He wished he were more familiar with the scriptures— something he meant to remedy. His finger slid down the page and across the verses until he found it.

"Isaiah 40:26. 'Lift up your eyes on high, and behold who hath created these things, that bringeth out their host by number: he calleth them all by names by the greatness of his might, for that he is strong in power; not one faileth.'"

He leaned against the back of the chair and let his gaze travel to the window. Beyond the pane, the starry host winked against the black backdrop in silent testimony of God's faithfulness. The very thought of being kept by a God who knew the precise location of each star and knew every one by name washed over him with soothing comfort. Those who put their trust in God were more important to Him than the stars. So if God cared enough to know the name of each star and secure it in place so that not a single star was missing, then surely God cared about him.

Everett propped an elbow on the arm of the chair and leaned his head into his palm. "God, I'm grateful for Your love. I just wish I understood why You've allowed the circumstances in my life to be what they are. How do I fit into Your plan? Can You use someone who looks like me?"

The Book in his lap coaxed his attention. His father had encouraged him to read through Proverbs. He found the place he'd left his bookmark in chapter 4. A frown tugged his brows together. So many of the verses talked about getting wisdom and understanding, but for the life of him, he couldn't understand why God wanted him to live with scars. Maybe if he just read on, the understanding would come later. He turned the page and hadn't read a half dozen verses when he backed up and reread a verse.

"My son, attend to my words; incline thine ear unto my sayings." He tipped his head back and stared at the ceiling. It wasn't hard to understand the first part. God instructed him to pay attention to His Word. The second half of the verse, however, gave him pause. "Incline my ear." He mulled over the words. "How does one incline the ear?"

Puzzling over God's choice of words, he rose and carried the lamp into the bedroom to prepare for bed. Tired as he was, his tumbling thoughts dogged him as he lay down on the feather tick. Despite shifting positions and determinedly keeping his eyes closed, he found that sleep eluded him. The clock on the bureau ticked away too many minutes to count as he lay awake. Surrendering, he opened his eyes and tucked his hands behind his head with a sigh.

A thin shaft of moonlight filtered through the curtain

and fell across the darkness of the room like an invitation from God, assuring Everett He was listening. Staring at the ceiling, he allowed his thoughts to wander. Not surprisingly, Tillie's image crept into his mind.

Father and Pearl seemed to think he should pursue a deeper relationship with Tillie. In order to do so, he'd have to put himself in a position of vulnerability. He doubted that he'd fooled either of them into believing he didn't care for Tillie. Here in the dark solitude of his bedroom, he admitted concern for her was only part of the reason he felt the need to put distance between them. Of course he didn't wish to hurt her, but if he were to be completely honest, he'd have to admit being vulnerable scared him.

He rolled over and studied the pale sliver of moonlight dimly illuminating the room. "God, I thought if I could live the life of a hermit and limit my contact with other people, I could create some kind of a private cocoon for myself—a niche in this world where people couldn't point and stare and laugh." An ache began to swell in his chest. "But it's lonely here. God, You know the smallest detail of my heart. Down deep, I really want to court Tillie. Sometimes I lay here in the dark and think of how it might be to watch her walk down the aisle to me and put her hand in mine. I can hide here where nobody knows my thoughts except You, and imagine how it might feel to kiss her."

Shoving back the covers, he sat up and swung his legs over the side of the bed. Elbows on knees, he ran both hands through his hair. "When it's daylight, I think how foolish it is to dream about such things. I can't lie to You. You know I'm not being noble by saying I don't want Tillie to be embarrassed or hurt, because that's only half the truth. I'm a coward, Lord. I'm afraid of the reactions of other people if I dared to behave as a normal man and ask a lovely young woman like Tillie if I could court her."

He stood and crossed the room, pushing the filmy curtain aside to look once again up at the stars that all had names. "God, help me grow my faith. You care for me like You care for the stars. I'm tired of being isolated and smothered. Give me the courage to step out and ask Tillie to accompany me to the harvest picnic." A warm breath of comfort caressed the side of his face—the side he continually tried to hide.

&

Everett didn't see Tillie for three whole days. Whether she left work earlier than usual or he closed the depot late, he wasn't sure. He'd rather have taken advantage of the privacy of their evening walks to ask if he could escort her to the picnic and barn dance. Perhaps this was part of God's answer to his prayer—nudging him to step away from his private cocoon.

Sunday morning dawned gray and gloomy with the scent of rain in the air. Everett paced the kitchen with a cup of coffee in hand, waiting to hear the church bell ring. He'd rehearsed what he planned to say a hundred times. Now he couldn't remember a single word. What if he tripped over his tongue and stammered? What if someone else overheard? He came to an abrupt halt. "What if she says no?"

The tolling of the church bell reached his ears. Before the final clang died away, Everett was down the back stairs and cutting through the alley. When he rounded the cedars at the edge of the churchyard, a few stragglers were still entering the church. Everett lingered behind the screen provided by the thick evergreens. There were no shadows, the sun remaining hidden behind a bank of heavy gray clouds.

The sound of hymn-singing floated on the air. Despite the gloomy day, hearts and voices were raised in worship. The thought bolstered his courage, and he straightened his shoulders, lifted his chin, and strode toward the church.

He slipped in during the last verse of "Come, Thou Fount of Every Blessing." *"Here's my heart, Lord; take and seal it. Seal it for Thy courts above."* The praise ringing within the walls of the church covered the sound of the door closing. He took his usual place at the back.

The hymn ended, and the congregation was seated—all except one small boy on the second pew from the rear who seemed determined to stand up on the bench despite his mother's efforts to tug him down on the seat. Finally the lad gave in to her admonitions and plopped down on the pew.

Pastor Witherspoon stepped into the pulpit. "Let's open our Bibles this morning and look at Paul's letter to the Colossians, chapter 3." The rustle of pages whispered across the room as folks found the text and settled in to listen to the preaching.

Before the pastor could begin reading, however, the little boy near the back stood up once again on the pew and turned, making faces at the people behind him. When the child's eyes locked with Everett's, the boy's stare widened. He pointed at Everett and yelled, "Mama! Look at that man! What's wrong with him?"

Nearly every head in the room turned, and all eyes followed the direction the lad pointed. Nausea twisted in Everett's gut, and his face flamed. Jerking his left hand up to cover his face, he ducked his head and leapt to his feet, his Bible falling on the floor. Two long strides took him from the bench to the door, where he yanked on the door handle and fled, leaving the gawkers behind.

❧

The ache in Tillie's chest prevented her from hearing most of what Pastor Witherspoon preached. Her heart ricocheted back and forth between anger at the child and at his mother for not keeping him under control, and grief for Everett. What kind of humiliation tormented him? Of course children said unkind things. She'd witnessed that earlier in the summer when the three youngsters from town mocked Everett in front of the freight depot. Oh, how she wished she could make him understand his scars didn't determine what kind of man he was, nor did they dampen her admiration of him.

She tried to discipline her mind to focus attention on the preacher but continually had to pull her thoughts back to the sermon. Finally, she gave up and closed her eyes, asking God what He might have her do. Should she go and find Everett and try to comfort him? That might make him assume that she pitied him. She'd seen firsthand how destructive pity could be, and she didn't wish that on Everett. No, her goal, with God's help, was to break down the wall he'd erected around himself and encourage him to seek God's will for his life. She spent the remainder of the service in prayer.

The last hymn was sung, the final prayer offered, and the service dismissed. As Tillie fell into line with her family, filing toward the door, she caught sight of Everett's Bible. Someone had picked it up and laid it on the bench. Her hand hesitated only a moment before reaching for the Book and tucking it into her shawl.

As she stepped to the open doorway, she scanned the churchyard even before she shook hands with the preacher. No sign of Everett. He might have simply gone home. Hubert and Pearl Behr stood in the middle of the yard, their searching eyes covering a wide circle. Tillie imagined they, too, hurt for Everett.

Da and Ma herded her siblings toward their wagon as a soft rumble of distant thunder rolled across the hills. She hurried to close the distance between her and her father. When he turned to look at her, she saw the same anguish in his eyes that she felt in her heart. He seemed to read her mind.

" 'Twas a hard thing for young Behr. But, daughter, he's goin' to hear such for the rest of his life. Either he learns to push it aside, or it'll do him in."

Tillie gave a slow nod. If anyone understood, Da did. "I don't pity him, Da, if that's what you're thinking. He must allow God to help him overcome the feelings of shame and embarrassment. I just want to let him know I still think he's a fine man."

Da's eyebrows arched, and he tilted his head up to look at the thick clouds roiling in the sky. Another gentle rumble of thunder sounded as if to punctuate his point. "And you feel the need to let him know that today, do you now?"

She saw him peek at her from the corner of his eye. He winked, and she threw her arms around his neck. "Yes, Da, I do. I don't know for certain where he is, but I suspect he might have gone down to the creek."

Da helped little Cory into the back of the wagon and latched the tailgate before turning back to Tillie. "And how do you plan to stay dry?"

She looked down at her shoe tips and gave a slight shake of her head before raising her head to give him a beseeching look. "Dry doesn't seem very important right now, Da."

He rolled his eyes heavenward. "I must be daft. I wonder if the good Lord gave my portion of common sense to somebody else. Go ahead. Find your young man."

Tillie didn't wait for him to change his mind, or for Ma to protest. She pulled her shawl snugly around her shoulders and scurried in the direction of the creek. Most of the other wagons had already departed, no doubt trying to beat the rain.

In the minute it took for her to run down the well-worn

path to the willow trees lining the creek, a few sprinkles began to fall. Puffing from exertion, Tillie pushed the willow withes aside, her eyes searching through the gloomy shadows for Everett's familiar silhouette. Perhaps he had more good sense than she and had headed for home.

She hiked up the creek bank, retracing her steps. Did she dare go knock on his door? That would certainly set the town tongues to wagging, and Da had admonished her about protecting her reputation. She blew out a huff through pursed lips. Just as she reached the edge of the churchyard once again, she caught a glimpse of movement beyond the cedar trees.

It's Everett.

Not knowing why, she stepped back, letting the cedar boughs conceal her as she watched to see where he'd go. He looked from left to right, apparently to satisfy himself that he was alone, and reentered the church. Indecision anchored Tillie in place. She longed to speak with him, but judging by his furtive glancing around the yard, he preferred solitude. An argument ensued within her. Should she leave him be or go reassure him? She didn't want him to feel abandoned, but she didn't want to intrude either.

"If I go in and sit with him, even if I don't say a word, at least he'll know I care."

Another rumble of thunder, this one a bit louder and longer, growled across the clouds. A soft, steady rain began, and she hastened her steps across the yard. The thought occurred to her that perhaps he merely came back for his Bible. Glancing to make certain the Book was protected from the rain by her shawl, she climbed the stairs and slipped in the door as the patter of rain increased.

There, at the front of the little sanctuary, Everett knelt. Her eyes traced the back of his head, bowed in prayer. How silly of her to think he'd feel abandoned. *He isn't alone. A child of God is never alone.* As she stood there, the words of his prayer reached her ears, and she felt like an interloper.

"I don't understand why You allowed me to live through that fire, God. Sometimes I think I'd rather be dead than look like this."

Tillie's throat tightened, and she put her hand over her mouth.

"But I know You don't make mistakes, so You must have a reason for these scars. I just wish I knew what that reason was."

Tillie laid his Bible on the back bench and started to leave, but the moment she shifted her weight, the floorboard under her foot gave a tiny squeak. She froze. If she moved, he'd know she'd been standing there eavesdropping. Holding her breath lest he hear that, too, she waited for the next roll of thunder and winced under an onslaught of guilt for listening to Everett pray.

"God, I'm tired of running and hiding, but the ugliness won't let me rest. I want to do something—be something— for You, but how can You use a broken vessel like me? Nobody wants to look at a man with a deformed face."

Tillie heard his voice grow tighter and more intense with each word.

"I keep telling myself it doesn't matter what other people think. It doesn't matter to You, God, but it does to me. I know it shouldn't, but it does. God, please—please make something beautiful of my life."

Everett's prayer stole Tillie's breath. She tightened her hand covering her mouth in an effort to prevent a sob from escaping. Even the years of watching people act repelled by her father's scars didn't prepare her for such a heartrending entreaty. Her eyes burned with unshed tears.

A flash of lightning lit the darkened interior of the church, followed seconds later by a booming crash of thunder. The noise echoed long enough for her to exit without being heard.

Something beautiful. His plea blew softly across her heart, mournful yet hopeful. She pulled her shawl up over her head and ran down the road, releasing the tears she'd held in check until now. When she passed the bend in the road and was quite sure Everett couldn't see her, she slowed her pace and plodded through the rain. Everett's heart-wrenching words echoed through her mind.

"I don't understand why You allowed me to live through that fire, God. Sometimes I think I'd rather be dead than look like this."

An unseen hand squeezed her heart. Tears continued to burn her eyes. "Please, God, let Everett hear Your voice. Fill him with an awareness of Your presence so he understands that his usefulness to You depends on his heart, not his appearance."

Tangled emotions stirred her stomach into turmoil as the rain dripped off the ends of her shawl, and the leaden sky wept in one accord with her.

nine

Tillie asked the two other women in the hotel kitchen to cover for her while she ran an errand. A twinge of guilt poked her as she scurried down the street toward the freight depot. It wasn't truly an errand, but her mission held an urgency that had kept her tossing and turning for the past three nights. If she hoped to get any sleep tonight, she'd best meet the situation head-on. Both determination and trepidation roiled in her stomach as she forced her feet to slow and walk sedately.

She paused a moment in front of the newspaper office, glancing at her reflection in the window. A few stray strands of hair had escaped their pins, and she tucked them back into place. With a rush of heat to her face, she hoped no one inside the office was watching her primp. Her gaze darted back and forth, and relief filled her when she saw the office seemed to be empty.

Just inside the window, a large calendar hung on the wall. Big black X's marked the passing of the days. Today's date, Thursday, the seventeenth of September, had yet to be marked off. Tillie took that as an encouragement—there was still time today to accomplish something significant. A tremor ran through her stomach as she considered her errand. She could still change her mind and return to the hotel. Momentary indecision held her in place.

Everett wasn't a coward—his heroic actions the day of the boardinghouse fire already proved that. Asking her if he could escort her to the harvest picnic and barn dance would take courage—he'd have to put aside his aversion to being seen in public. But how long should she wait for him to gather that courage?

She sucked in a fortifying breath. Her intentions might not be considered proper, especially back east where Everett came from, but if she let many more days pass without her planned discussion with him, her only opportunity might slip through her fingers. Resolve straightened her shoulders, and she continued down the boardwalk. The small sign on the door of the freight office declared the business open. She stepped inside, but instead of encountering Everett, Ben stood at the front counter. The moment he saw her, he swept his hat off.

"Miss Tillie." Ben's lopsided smile accentuated his deep brown eyes. He ran his hand over his head, smoothing out unruly hair the same color as a wheat field ripe for harvest. "It's sure nice to see you in the middle of the week instead of just on Sunday." He dusted off his shirt and wiped his hands on the seat of his pants.

A bit of the determination that had propelled her down the boardwalk seeped out of her. "H–hello, Ben."

Ben hung his hat on a nail stuck in the wall behind him. "It's been kind of hard to talk to you at church, Miss Tillie. You're always hurrying off somewhere." He shuffled his boot against the corner of the counter. "I'd like to talk to you, if you have a minute."

Tillie clasped her hands tightly in front of her waist. She hated to admit it, but she hadn't given Ben much of a chance for fellowshipping either before or after church. He always seemed to be standing there in the churchyard, waiting to help her down from her family's wagon on Sunday mornings. In her haste today, she'd not stopped to think that she'd likely run into Ben at the depot. Now he stood before her waiting for a reply.

She gave him an apologetic smile. "I'm sorry, Ben. I didn't mean to be rude." She slid a surreptitious glance beyond Ben's shoulder toward the door to the rear office, wondering if Everett could hear their conversation. "The other ladies in the hotel kitchen are expecting me back in a few minutes, so I really can't linger."

Ben took a step forward. The hopeful expression on his face pricked her. She'd never noticed before the depth of his eyes. There was something warm and welcoming about them. She could well imagine some young lady falling beneath their spell and sighing with contentment in their captivity. The thought brought a tiny smile to her lips.

Ben's hands fumbled, and he stuck one hand in his pocket as if he didn't know what else to do with it. "This won't take long, Tillie. I—I was just wondering if you planned on going to the harvest picnic and the barn dance. I mean, I didn't know if"—he glanced toward Everett's office door—"anyone had asked you yet."

Tillie drew in a breath and held it. She didn't want to hurt Ben's feelings. She liked Ben. He was a pleasant fellow, honest, hardworking, and polite, but his invitation caught her off balance. Her purpose in taking time away from her lunch break had everything to do with the picnic and dance. In fact, her planned errand included something positively scandalous and bold. She intended to march straight into Everett's office and ask him herself. But she hadn't planned on running into Ben.

She could honestly say that she'd prayed about it. Most of the nighttime hours she'd spent tossing and turning had been filled with whispered prayers. In spite of her repeated petitions, she hadn't felt the affirmation she'd sought. Impatience chewed at her good sense. Waiting had always been difficult for her, but how long did God intend for her to wait on His answer? A flash of caution shook her. She truly didn't have peace over what she was about to do. Maybe encountering Ben was God's way of stopping her from making a huge mistake.

Apparently, her hesitation communicated indecision to Ben. "Well, you think on it a spell, Miss Tillie. Guess I don't need an answer right now. But since the picnic's just a little over a week away. . ." He didn't need to finish the sentence, and Tillie knew she wasn't being fair to make him wait for an answer. If Everett had asked her weeks ago when she'd first hinted about it, she wouldn't be in this predicament. Because of his reticence, she found herself putting Ben off.

She looked down at her entwined fingers. "Ben, I. . ."

Ben gave her another lopsided smile with a small sigh of resignation. His eyes traveled again to the door of the inner office and back to her, like he read her mind. "I know, Miss Tillie. I was just hoping is all. Maybe I'll see you there." He retrieved his hat and plopped it back on his head, tugging at the brim. "Good day, Miss Tillie." He stepped out the door, leaving it standing open, and ambled across the street.

Guilt skewered her as she watched Ben retreating toward the livery with shoulders slumped, and it was all Everett's fault. He'd had plenty of opportunity to ask her. She blew out a pent-up breath and raised her hand to knock on the office door, only to have the door open and her knuckles collide with the very man she came to see.

"Whoa." Everett caught her hand, his fingers wrapping around hers for the space of two heartbeats. A tingle shot up her arm and accelerated her pulse. He abruptly released her fingers and yanked his hand up to cover his face.

He took a step backward. "Are you all right?"

At the moment, she wasn't certain how to answer that question. Their impromptu meeting in the doorway had left her none the worse for wear on the outside, but a war was raging on the inside. She narrowed her eyes and plunked both hands on her hips.

"Everett Behr!"

An expression of expectation arched his eyebrows. "Yes?"

She marched past him into the office, vaguely aware of the dimmed light with the window shade partially pulled down. She sat on a chair only to bounce back up again an instant later and pace across the room. Exasperation curled her fingers into fists held tightly to her sides in an effort to keep them from reaching out and grabbing Everett's hand away from his face.

"Sometimes you make me so angry!"

Mild surprise flitted across his face, at least the part of his face she could see. "What have I done?"

Irritation climbed up her frame and spilled over. "Nothing. That's just the problem."

"Oh?" His mouth tipped into a half smile.

His quiet amusement rankled her even further. A fleeting nudge signaled her to hold her tongue and her temper, but she shoved it away and barged ahead. She thrust both hands out, palms up, fingers splayed. "Everett Behr, you've got to be the most aggravating, pigheaded, prickly man I've ever met!"

He tucked his chin back a bit and blinked. "I beg your pardon?"

"Argh!" She spun around and turned her back to him. *Count to ten before you say anything else.* "You—you—" she sputtered. *"Be ye kind one to another, tenderhearted. . . ."* She whirled back around. "You are a stubborn man."

"Mm. I've been called worse." He reclined against the edge of the desk, seemingly unperturbed by her outburst. "I'm having a little difficulty, however, understanding why you've taken the time to come all the way over here just to tell me I'm stubborn."

"And aggravating and pigheaded!"

He covered his mouth with his hand and muffled a cough. "And prickly." He folded his arms across his chest. "Would you mind telling me what this is all about?"

She could have sworn she heard a grin in his voice. Tears threatened to embarrass her, but she clamped her teeth together and swallowed hard. She took in his familiar form, swathed in shadows as always. How her heart longed to draw him out of those shadows.

"Everett, why can't you see yourself for the man you are? The man on the inside. Because that's the man I see."

His posture stiffened, and a hint of sarcasm threaded his tone. "You must not be looking hard enough."

"You won't let me." She thrust her hands in the air in frustration. "Every time I see you, you either turn away or cover your face. You hide in the shadows and refuse to let anyone come close. I thought we were friends, Everett. No, more than just friends. At least I'd hoped so. But if you keep hiding behind this wall you've erected around yourself, how will I ever know for sure?"

He unfolded his arms and braced his palms against the desk, lowering his chin and staring at the floor. "Tillie, open your eyes. You say you see me for what I am. Well, what I am is ugly. I can't be what you want me to be, and that's the reality of it." He turned and walked around the other side of the desk. "I happen to know Ben was planning on asking you to the picnic and barn dance."

The tears that tried to choke her earlier snuck back into her throat. "He did."

"So are you going?"

"I don't know."

Everett blew out a breath, sounding as exasperated as she. "What do you mean you don't know? What are you waiting for?"

"I was waiting—hoping—that you. . ." Her original plan seemed to be crumbling at her feet.

"No, Tillie. I can't." His words sounded frozen.

She drew herself up and raised her chin. "Well, I came to tell you there isn't a man in this town who appeals to me as much as you do."

Everett shook his head. "Tillie, you aren't listening. You're being foolish, making Ben wait for an answer."

"So it's foolish I am, is it?" She plopped both fists on her hips. "I suppose I've been foolish to go walking with you in the evening. Have I been foolish to sit by the creek and share personal thoughts and cares?" Her voice rose in pitch as her throat began to tighten. "Are you telling me I've been foolish to pray for you?"

With every word she came closer until they were glaring at each other across the desk. She planted her palms on the desk and leaned in. "For your information, I do know my own mind and heart, but I'm beginning to doubt if you've ever listened to your heart. I think you've lied to yourself. You've talked yourself into believing you aren't good enough for polite company. Well, let me tell you something, Mr. Everett Behr. You're wrong."

Characteristically, Everett turned away. With his back to her, he stepped to the window and tugged the shade, darkening the room a bit more. "Tillie, stop this. Go back to the hotel. We both have work to do."

His cool dismissal crippled her. She tried to draw in a deep breath, but her lungs rebelled. "So that's it? That's all you have to say?"

He opened a file drawer and pulled out some papers,

flipping through them as though they were of great importance. "Go to the picnic with Ben."

His reply stung. This wasn't the same Everett with whom she'd spent leisurely evening hours, walking and sharing her thoughts. In fact, the man in front of her now seemed more like the old Everett, the one who didn't care who he hurt. The former arrogance was missing, but the same coldness she remembered cloaked him once more. She huffed out a stiff breath. "Maybe I will."

"Good," he said, his quiet voice taking on a cynical tone as he reached for another file. "It's about time you took my advice."

This wasn't turning out the way she'd planned at all, and it was her own fault. She'd allowed her temper to break its restraints and run amok, instead of letting compassion control her. The tears finally won the battle and slid silently down her cheeks.

&

Everett's acerbic tone surprised even him. He didn't relish telling her to accept Ben's invitation. The very words carved another scar—this one across his heart. But what else could he do? Tillie had accused him of being pigheaded, but he suspected she could match him stubborn for stubborn. There was no other choice but to make her angry enough with him that she'd want to seek other companionship. Her kindness and compassion were so clearly etched into her words and actions that he'd seen the reason she had reached out to him from the very beginning. As much as he'd enjoyed her friendship, it was time for her to move on.

He listened for her stomping footsteps retreating, punctuated by the slamming of the door, but he heard neither. When he turned, she was still standing there, but the picture she made wasn't at all what he anticipated. He expected her anger. He didn't expect her tears.

An unseen fist belted him in the stomach and sent a bitter lance careening through his chest, robbing his breath. His fingers curled tightly around the papers in his hand. This was wrong. He never intended for Tillie to be hurt by his tactics. She deserved to find a man who could love her and make her proud of him. A man with whom she could spend the rest of her life. Not someone like him.

God must have intended for him to live a solitary life. Why else would He allow the scars? If he could survive the pain of being burned, then surely he could survive the pain of being alone.

But Tillie. . .ah, sweet Tillie. *Girl, don't you know I'm doing this for you?* A raw ache twisted and seared his stomach at the thought of pushing her away. He'd carefully designed his words to make her just angry enough that she'd direct her affections elsewhere. Only knowing she would eventually find the man God intended for her enabled him to sever their friendship. A startled tremor rattled him. What he felt for Tillie wasn't friendship, and he could no longer remain in her presence and pretend that was all he wanted.

His gaze fastened onto the tear sliding down her cheek and dripping off her chin. This wasn't turning out the way he'd planned, and self-loathing filled him to think he'd made her cry. But if he relented now, the carefully laid groundwork would be destroyed.

"I'm sorry, Tillie, but it's best this way."

She remained motionless, as though her feet were nailed to the floor. The longer she stood there, the more difficult it was for him to draw breath. His arms ached to hold her close. He longed to apologize for causing her pain and whisper soothing words of comfort. But the words knotted together in his throat. What would it take to get her to leave?

He stiffened his spine and sat at his desk, spreading papers in front of him and studying them with rapt attention. The words and figures blurred and ran together, but he kept his eyes fixed. *Please, God, just let her leave. I'm sorry I had to be mean to her, but she'll be happier in the days to come.*

Finally, a soft sigh reached his ears, but it hit like Cully's hammer.

"I'm sorry, too, Everett. I wanted to make you see. . . . But I realize now I was trying to do God's job for Him. He's trying to tell you something, Everett, and it's up to you whether or not you listen. I won't stop praying for you."

The sound he thought he'd wanted to hear, her footsteps exiting the office, echoed in his heart like a funeral dirge. It made little sense now to pray that what he'd done was right. It was done, and Tillie very likely would never be back.

He propped his elbows on the desk and lowered his head to his hands. "God, please wrap her in Your comfort." He sat thus for a long time. When he finally raised his head and looked at the papers on the desk before him, he realized they were all upside down, a painfully familiar perspective.

ten

The pungent scent of autumn greeted Everett when he stepped out his door. He breathed deeply of the crisp air, more for fortification than enjoyment of the season. Instead of waiting until he heard the church bell ring this morning, a motivation he couldn't explain drove him to leave for church early. What was the point? It wasn't as if he planned to talk to anyone. A battle of inclinations fought a tug-of-war in his chest. He both relished and dreaded seeing Tillie.

Perturbed at his own fickleness, he proceeded down the back stairs and walked resolutely through the alley to the well-worn path leading to the thick cedars that surrounded the churchyard. He could see several wagons and buggies arriving, folks calling out greetings to each other, parents tugging at their children in a vain attempt to keep them clean. Their cheerfulness gnawed at him. Even the cornflower-blue sky lent a sharp contrast to his mood. If he'd had the privilege of choosing the day's colors, a dark, gloomy sky layered with gray clouds matched his spirit better than the sunny morning with tinges of gold, russet, and red highlighting the trees.

Everett stepped closer but remained in the shelter of the cedars. Ben Kiefer arrived on foot and shook hands with a few of the other men. Ben attended church most Sundays, but today his employee sported a tie. And was that a new shirt? Ben rubbed the tops of his boots on the backs of his pant legs and stood, shifting his weight from one foot to the other, glancing repeatedly to the road coming into town. A growl rumbled in Everett's throat, but he pushed it down.

Another wagon pulled into the yard, this one carrying Everett's father and Pearl. His gaze lingered on the pair. Perhaps today wasn't a good time to contemplate the way God had blessed his father, leading him to find love again late in life. He didn't begrudge his father the happiness, but how he longed to know that kind of happiness for himself. A twinge of envy pinched Everett as he watched the solicitous manner in which the elder Behr aided his bride down from the wagon, holding her shawl for her and offering his arm as they made their way toward the church. A fresh pang of loneliness sliced through him, and a bitter thought taunted him. God would have to send a blind woman for him to be so blessed.

"Halloo, Hubert and Pearl. A fine Lord's day to ye." The ringing voice yanked Everett's attention back to the churchyard activity. Timothy O'Dell waved from the wagon seat as he pulled his team to a stop and set the brake. Before Everett could blink, Ben Kiefer was beside the O'Dell wagon, reaching to take Tillie's hand and help her down.

Everett's jaw tightened. What was the strange sensation whirling in his stomach? If he had to put a title to it, might it be jealousy? That was ludicrous. Such an emotion served no purpose, save stirring a slightly nauseous wave rising within him.

Ben removed his hat and ran a hand over his head to smooth his already neatly combed hair. He nodded and spoke briefly to Tillie's parents. But as the rest of her family made their way into the church, Tillie remained beside the wagon with Ben. Everett turned his head to incline his ear toward the two, but between the breeze rustling the leaves, a nearby dog barking, and a flock of noisy crows squabbling over a few grains of corn next to the mill, he couldn't make out a word they said to each other. Judging by the red stain on Ben's face, they weren't discussing the weather.

The church bell began to ring, and the handful of people who lingered in the churchyard scurried toward the front door. Except Ben and Tillie. They remained in place, conversing about something. Tillie nodded her head, and a pleased smile stretched across Ben's face. Then he said something that made Tillie laugh. Everett's breath caught, and for a moment he feared he might give away his hiding place by coughing. But no cough could make it past the stranglehold in his throat when Ben offered his arm to Tillie and she slipped her arm through his—just like his father did with Pearl.

Whatever he'd eaten for breakfast that morning sat like lead in his stomach. An image formed in his mind and mocked him with the relentless persistence of a wood-boring insect. What if, from his usual seat against the back wall of the church, he had to look at Ben and Tillie sitting side by side in a pew ahead of him, sharing a hymnbook? At the moment, it mattered little how often he'd tried to encourage Tillie to welcome Ben's attention. The reality of it coming to fruition slammed into him like a locomotive.

He turned and strode away, no destination in mind. He simply knew he wasn't ready to watch his own plan unfold before him.

"I know it's for the best, Lord. I just wasn't prepared for the way it would make me feel."

A dozen contradictions collided in his head, good sense conflicting with paradox. He kept walking until he reached the familiar screen of willow branches, the same ones among which he and Tillie had strolled and talked. In this very spot he'd first realized how easy Tillie was to talk to. Sitting on this rock, the two of them had dangled their feet in the creek and tried to improvise a harmony to "Rock of Ages." They'd shared thoughts, stories, and laughter.

Everett sat down on the rock. It was too chilly to dip his feet in the creek, but he closed his eyes, and despite his glum mood, a smile found his lips when he remembered the twinkle in Tillie's eyes when she first suggested they do so. He picked up a round, flat stone and skipped it across the water. The memory of her laughter, sweeter than the most haunting concerto, accompanied the stone as it flirted with the water, only to be consumed by it.

Missing church saddened him. Learning scripture and listening to the pastor's practical lessons, the joy of growing stronger in his faith and closer to his Lord, had become a delight. More than that, his awareness of God's presence had begun to expand into an appetite he couldn't satisfy. He hungered to know more of his God, even if he couldn't always understand His ways. As he cast a slow scan around him, the trees and grasses waving in the breeze, the music of the water flowing over the rocks, even the dance of the butterflies, all lent themselves to an air of worship. He knew, in the coming weeks, he'd fortify himself and step into church again, even if it meant seeing Ben and Tillie together. Today he would praise God right here. The cathedral God Himself created would serve as his altar. He lifted his face and felt the warmth of the sun as he opened his mouth and sang.

"Rock of Ages, cleft for me; let me hide myself in Thee." He halted in the middle of the verse. He'd hidden in the shadows and behind his hand, pulled his hat down low on his face, turned away from staring eyes, and sequestered himself. He'd searched for every conceivable place to hide except in Christ.

"How could I not have seen it before, Lord? You are my Rock, and You can shelter me in Your hiding place better

than any device on this earth. Let me hide myself in Thee."
Letting God minister to him in solitude this day was exactly
what his raw heart needed.

"God, I feel so hollow inside. As difficult as it is to accept,
I know Tillie isn't the one to fill the emptiness. But if I can
hide in You, then I know You can fill those barren places
with Yourself."

He rose and began walking with no thought of direction,
cresting hills and crossing meadows, climbing rocks and
hiking up ridges. He continued until his legs begged for rest.
Now surrounded by mostly wooded hills, he found a shady
place near some rocks and stretched out in the grass.

❧

The moment the pastor pronounced the final amen, Tillie
turned to look behind her. Of course Everett wasn't there.
He always slipped out before the end of the service. But
during the singing, she'd sneaked a few brief glances, and his
usual spot remained vacant. She hoped he wasn't ill. Sorrow
stung her. What if he'd chosen to stay out of church? She
hadn't been able to get his plea for God to make something
beautiful of his life out of her mind. That wasn't the only
thing she couldn't forget. She could still hear his voice—like
the sound the ice on the pond made in early winter when
someone tried to step on it before it was strong enough. An
ominous groan. *"I'm sorry, Tillie, but it's best this way."*

"Are you looking for something, Miss Tillie?" Ben's warm
eyes glanced down at her and then followed the same path
hers had just taken across the room.

She gulped and forced a smile. "I was hoping to see
my friend Tessa Maxwell." It wasn't a lie. She did want to
speak to Tessa. She needed her friend's sympathetic ear.
She spotted Tessa across the crowded chapel as folks were
moving toward the door. It didn't seem likely she'd get a

chance for a private talk with Tessa today, but maybe they could plan to get together later in the week. Her heart was sore and full of regret. A chat with Tessa usually made her feel better, but this time she wasn't sure anything could soothe her.

They moved along with the exiting worshippers. Ahead of her, Da and Ma gathered the young ones before they had a chance to scatter. Ben shook hands with the preacher and then took her hand as she descended the stairs. Tillie sent another surreptitious glance, this time around the churchyard. Everett was nowhere to be seen, but she did catch a glimpse of Hubert helping Pearl into their wagon.

"Please excuse me, Ben. There's someone I need to catch before they leave."

Ben nodded and tipped his hat like a perfect gentleman, but she didn't wait for his reply. Dodging around some children playing tag, she hurried toward Hubert and Pearl's wagon.

"Pearl." She called out and waved a hand to stop them.

"Good morning, Tillie." Pearl smiled down from her perch on the wagon seat. "I wondered if we'd get a chance to speak."

Tillie wasn't unaware of the heads turning to take note of her sitting with Ben in church. No doubt the town gossipers would have them engaged by nightfall. Pearl didn't gossip, but Tillie was certain she wondered about Ben. She'd have time later to explain that Ben was nothing more than a friend. At the moment, she had a much more pressing question on her mind.

"I didn't see Everett this morning. Do you know why he's not here?"

Pearl turned to look at her husband and then back at Tillie. "We were hoping you would know."

Tillie shook her head. "I haven't seen him for a few days."

She dropped her gaze to her fingers clutching the ends of her shawl. "We. . .had words. I went by the depot a few days ago, and we argued." She looked back at Pearl and Hubert. "I hope he hasn't stayed away from church because of me."

Pearl glanced at her husband, who gave Tillie a grand-fatherly smile. "Everett is a big boy. He makes his own decisions. It's best we leave him alone for a while until he feels like talking."

They bid each other good-bye, and Tillie stepped back as the wagon rolled away. She scanned the yard again in search of Tessa and found her with Gideon and their little daughter talking to one of the area ranchers. A quick glance toward her family's wagon revealed Ben standing there talking to Da. A fleeting curiosity skittered through her as she speculated over the topic of their conversation. She dismissed it as inconsequential.

Hurrying across the yard, she touched Tessa's shoulder. Her friend greeted her with a smile and a hug.

"We went out to Fletcher Hamilton's ranch last week to deliver a horse, and Fletcher was trying to interest Gideon in the sheep. Susan was fascinated by the woolies." Tessa tilted her head toward her husband and the rancher. "Looks like the little imp is trying to talk her daddy into going back for another visit."

Despite her melancholy, Tillie couldn't help but smile at the tiny girl holding her father's hand. When she looked up, Tessa was studying her. "I see pain in those eyes. Is something wrong?"

Tessa's question nearly unleashed the tears she'd been holding at bay for days. "Oh, Tessa, I think I've ruined everything. Everett and I argued, and it was my fault."

Her friend gave her a gentle smile. "It takes two people to argue."

Tillie shrugged. "Maybe. But what if he never wants to see me again? I don't know if I could stand that."

Tessa's eyebrows arched along with the intensity of her voice. "You're in love with him." She quickly slipped her hand over her mouth and glanced left and right, her gaze lingering past Tillie's shoulder.

Tillie followed Tessa's line of sight and turned to find Ben standing behind her, crushing the brim of his hat in his curled fist. The peculiar expression in his eyes indicated he'd heard Tessa's declaration, but to his credit, he didn't comment on it.

"Miss Tillie, would you do me the honor of allowing me to walk you home? I already asked your pa, and he said it was all right."

Tessa reached to lay a gloved hand on Tillie's arm. "Go ahead. We'll talk later. Can you come for tea this week?"

Tillie nodded numbly. Mortification shot up her spine at the thought of Ben overhearing her conversation with Tessa. She liked Ben—even believed him a suitable candidate as a beau. When Everett had told her it was time she took his advice and accepted Ben, maybe he'd given that advice in a big brotherly way. The thought wounded her. She already had brothers, and what she felt for Everett had nothing to do with sibling affection. But perhaps he was right. She peered up at Ben, searching for those qualities Everett had tried to point out.

"That's very kind of you, Ben."

He took her hand and tucked it in the crook of his elbow. "It's a beautiful day. Just right for taking a walk."

She forced a smile, and they set off down the road—the same road Everett had walked with her that first evening when the crickets and whippoorwills accompanied them.

✦

Everett opened his eyes, surrounded by the sweet scent

of meadow grass and autumn leaves. When the breeze died momentarily, he heard a faint gurgling sound. Pushing himself up to a sitting position, he found a tiny trickle of water seeping from between the rocks a few feet away. A smile found his lips as he recalled the scripture he'd read from Proverbs about cold water to a thirsty soul. God found a way to minister to him even when he wasn't looking for it. He scooted over and cupped his hand, capturing the flow and lifting it to his mouth. As he expected, the water was pure and sweet.

Everett carried handfuls of water to his lips and satisfied his thirst, then wiped his sleeve across his face. Dabbling his fingers in the cold spring, his thoughts wandered to Tillie and the times they'd enjoyed the creek water flowing over their toes. This tiny rivulet meandered down the slope, where it fed into a small branch that ran alongside the base of the hill. Everett assumed the branch emptied into Willow Creek. He wondered if Tillie knew about this spring. A tempting thought to bring her to this place taunted him, but he shook his head at the foolishness of the idea.

Dropping to his knees in the thick grass beside the spring, he tilted his head back and groaned to his heavenly Father. "God, I know it can never be. Please take these feelings for Tillie away from me. You are the God of all comfort. Every need I have, You've supplied. Father, I beg You to fill the dry, empty places of my soul with Your presence. Teach me to hide in You. I know You'll take care of Tillie. Truly, my desire is for her to be happy, and that can't happen with me. So, Lord, bring her happiness in whatever way You think is best."

He rose and began walking down the slope in the direction of town. He might not have worshipped within the walls of the church this day, but he'd spent time at God's footstool and had drunk in His refreshing presence. Grateful for the way God ministered to his spirit, he was determined to exercise his faith and leave the outcome to the One who gave cold water to his thirsty soul.

The sun was high overhead as he cut through the thick woods and crossed over grassy hills. The earlier nip in the air gave way to the warming rays. Everett removed his coat and loosened his tie. During the many evening walks he'd taken with Tillie over the past few months, he'd discovered he loved walking. Of course, walking with Tillie was different. They'd shared so much as they strolled among the willows. But Everett found this day's solitude was not lonely. His walking partner today was God.

Refreshed by the communion he'd shared with his heavenly Father, he hiked up a rise and paused. Below, the road that led to town wove through cornfields and grazing pastures. A couple walked down the road. The young lady held a black book—a Bible?—snugly against her, and they appeared to be walking home from church. The lady's familiar honey-blond hair was pinned up and tied with a green ribbon. *Tillie and Ben.*

Ben stopped and bent to pick up a few colorful autumn leaves, and Tillie pointed across the meadow to a stand of maples aflame in seasonal dress. They appeared to be enjoying each other's company. Neither of them looked in Everett's direction.

The promise of God's comfort and hiding place washed over him once again. So this was His answer. An ache stole into the pit of his stomach, but he knew even then that God wouldn't leave him alone.

eleven

Amusement teased the corners of Tillie's lips as she listened to Tessa patiently explain to her little daughter that they weren't going to see the lambs today. Little Susan's bottom lip pooched out, and her blue eyes filled. Tessa appeased her with a cookie.

"She sounds like Cory when he's got his mind made up about something." Tillie stroked the child's hair.

Tessa sighed. "Susan, take your dolly and put her down for a nap. If she doesn't go to sleep, you might have to lie down beside her until she does."

Susan cradled her rag doll in her arms and trotted off toward the bedroom, crooning to her baby. As soon as she was out of earshot, Tessa chuckled.

"Gideon's thinking about purchasing a half dozen head of sheep from Fletcher, but he hasn't had time to go back out to the Hamilton ranch. When we were there last week, Susan got a look at the new lambs, and that's all she's talked about ever since." Tessa shook her head and stirred a spoonful of sugar into her cup.

Tillie took a sip of tea and bit into a cookie. The little girl was so appealing her parents surely must be hard-pressed to say no. A wistful pining squeezed her, and for the space of a heartbeat she experienced a tug of envy.

"But you didn't come over here to talk about Susan and the lambs."

Tillie ran her finger around the rim of her teacup and lifted her shoulders. "Truly? I'm not sure what I came to talk about." She didn't look at Tessa, but she knew her friend was smiling.

"Am I safe in assuming this is about Everett?"

Hearing his name spoken sent an arrow of regret through her breast. "Tessa, all I wanted was for God to use me. I'd hoped Everett would see himself the way God does. Just because he's scarred doesn't mean he has to spend the rest of his life hiding from people."

"That doesn't sound like a bad thing." Tessa's expression indicated she didn't understand Tillie's low spirits. "Why are you so melancholy? Won't Everett listen to you?"

Tillie rose from her chair and crossed the kitchen to look out the window. The trees had begun to give up their summer green in exchange for autumn yellows, russets, and oranges—changes ushered in by the season—a gift from God's own hand. Strange, how such woeful thoughts could dim the brilliance of the Lord's blessings.

"Everett and I, well. . .we were seeing each other. Going for walks and sitting by the creek in the evening after work." The sweetness of the memories they'd made together ached within her, especially since she feared those memories might turn bitter. She turned and walked back to the table where Tessa sat. "Everett seemed so much more relaxed in the evening— you know, as it was getting dark. We'd talk and laugh."

Tessa tipped her head to one side. "You *were* seeing each other?"

Tillie nodded, her fingers tracing the back of the chair. "Sometimes two or three times a week. I enjoyed our time together so much, and I thought Everett did, too. He told me funny stories about the stray cat he adopted, and I told him about my little brothers' adventures. We discussed Pastor Witherspoon's sermons, and sometimes we even sang whatever hymns came to mind. Being with him felt so right."

She slid back down on the chair she had vacated. "Then he started acting. . .different."

"Different how?"

The words to describe the way Everett seemed to pull away failed her, and she wasn't certain she even wanted to give definition to the fracture. If she could put it into words, did that make it so? How could she and Everett rediscover the closeness they'd shared? Was she simply supposed to accept the distance between them as inevitable and move on? She shook her head, stubbornness stiffening her spine.

"It was because of his scars—I'm sure of it. You know how he always pulls his hat lower or brings his hand up to hide his face?" She raised her hand and covered the right side of her own face, imitating Everett's habit. "Every time he does that, it breaks my heart. Why can't he see that his scars aren't important? Not to God, and not to—"

One corner of Tessa's mouth tipped up. "Not to you? So was I right? Are you in love with him?"

Oh, how she wanted to shout yes—yes, she was in love with Everett. Instead she looked away. "It doesn't matter. I've ruined everything."

Tessa gave a soft snort. "How do you figure that?"

"Because I did the exact opposite of what I told Everett he should do." She tipped her head back and slid her eyes shut. "He and I talked about trust one evening, and I said how people should wait on God and let Him lead in situations that are too difficult to handle." She leaned forward and popped her eyes open again. "So what did I do? Things weren't going the way I wanted, so I barged ahead and took matters into my own hands."

She stood again and began to pace, spilling out the story of her visit to the freight office and her argument with Everett. "We haven't seen each other for more than a week. He's cut off our friendship. He doesn't want anything to do with me, and he thinks I'm foolish."

Tessa rose and crossed the room, slipping an arm around Tillie. "You still haven't answered my question. Are you in love with him?"

Her friend's tender prodding released her hold on her emotions, and the tears began to flow. She nodded. "But it doesn't matter what I feel. Everett has pushed me toward Ben and shut me out." She wiped the moisture from her face.

"Pushed you toward Ben? What do you mean?"

Tillie sighed. "Ben asked me to the picnic, and Everett kept telling me I should go with him. All I wanted to do was make Everett see that his scars don't change the man he is. But I've made such a mess of things. Why didn't I wait on God?"

࿐

Everett handed his father the letter from Grandfather's attorney and watched as he read it. The empty mercantile gave them a private moment to discuss the surprise Everett had received in the mail. "The last thing I expected was an offer from one of Grandfather's former business constituents."

His father laid the missive on the counter and scrunched his thick eyebrows together. "After the estate was settled and the creditors paid off, I assumed you'd never hear from any of those people again." He played with one end of his mustache. "I'm guessing this man respected the way you handled the settlement, since he says he's"—Father glanced down at the paper and ran his finger across one of the inked lines—"looking for a dependable man of integrity to manage his financial interests." He blew out a soft sigh. "Have you decided what you're going to do?"

Everett shook his head. "Grandfather's attorney is a very trustworthy man, so I don't doubt the validity of the offer." He ran his hand through his hair. "If I'd received this letter last year, I wouldn't have hesitated to respond in the affirmative."

Father pulled the pencil from behind his ear. "The salary this man is proposing would certainly allow you to live quite comfortably."

If Everett had learned anything over the past year, it was that money wasn't everything. "I agree the offer is rather lucrative, but the money isn't that important." He picked up the letter and reread the description of everything the job entailed: overseeing accounts and expenditures, and keeping precise records, much like a comptroller. "The thing that attracts me most is having little contact with people other than the owner of the company. This is a job I could do behind a closed door."

The furrow between his father's brows deepened. "Is that truly what you want?"

Everett hated the indecision that lifted his shoulders in an uncertain shrug. "In the past few months, I've established myself as a businessman, and people seem to appreciate the service I provide. But now. . ."

His father didn't press him to finish his thought. The elder Behr's insightful eyes fastened on him. The growing bond between them coaxed Everett to allow transparency.

"When I first arrived in Willow Creek, I couldn't imagine myself living here. But after the fire. . .and the scars. . .I couldn't imagine going back to live in Baltimore, looking the way I do. Life in Willow Creek is simple. I thought I no longer had the choice of hoping for anything more."

A hint of sorrow clouded his father's eyes. "I want to see you happy, son, but I'd be less than honest if I didn't express my desire for you to stay in Willow Creek." Father stroked his whiskered chin. "What about your business? Do you think you could find a buyer?"

Everett shrugged. "I might talk to Ben about it."

"Does Ben have the capital?"

"I doubt it, but we could draw up an agreement whereby he could send me payments." He steeled himself against the pain that clawed at him. If Ben bought the freight operation, he'd have the means to support Tillie comfortably.

His father cleared his throat. "Is there another reason you're considering this offer? Does this have anything to do with Tillie?"

Everett thought his friendship with Tillie a healthy thing until his feelings toward her changed. Now he knew better. Since Tillie had finally taken his advice and accepted Ben's attention, seeing the two of them together was far more painful than he'd anticipated. At least if he moved back to Baltimore, he wouldn't have to watch Tillie being courted by another man. His father had seen through the smoke and nailed the real reason the Baltimore offer was so tempting.

"I'd like your opinion, Father."

No smile tweaked his father's mustache. "Son, please don't make up your mind yet. Pray about this. God will never start something in your life that He doesn't intend to finish." He squeezed his son's shoulder. "You know I want you to stay, but *you* must weigh the reasons you're considering this move. My opinion isn't the one that counts."

Everett's fingers itched to take up paper and pen and reply to the attorney's letter, but Father's advice was wise. It had to be for the right reasons. He folded the letter and tucked it into his pocket. Before he could accept this offer, he needed to spend some time in serious thought. . .and prayer.

৯

Everett wrestled for three days trying to compose a reply to the letter, only to crumple countless pages of stationery. During his time of prayer, he only heard one word from God: *"Wait."*

With Ben out on a delivery, Everett had to keep the door to his inner office open so he'd hear if a customer came in. He bent his head over the invoices on his desk and tried to concentrate on the figures, but the letter in his desk drawer fought for his attention.

The outside door opened, and Everett glanced up. A gust of wind accompanied a gentleman into the outer office, and from his vantage point in the shadowed inner office, Everett recognized Tillie's father. He rose from behind his desk and stepped to the doorway, his hand jerking up and then hesitating. Would Mr. O'Dell find his maneuver to conceal his scars offensive? He dropped his hand to his side.

"Good afternoon, sir. You're Mr. O'Dell, are you not?"

The Irishman removed his hat and raised his chin a bit, exposing his own facial scar to the light pouring in from the open door. "That I am, young fella."

While Everett could detect a lilt in Tillie's speech from time to time, Mr. O'Dell's brogue was much more pronounced. He could see where Tillie got her green eyes. If he didn't miss his guess, he was about to find out where she got her stubbornness as well.

Everett stepped into the front portion of the office. "What can I do for you, Mr. O'Dell?"

The man leveled a look at Everett that he could have sworn went all the way through to his back collar button. "Thought I'd see if you had time for a wee chat." Without waiting for Everett's reply, O'Dell continued, "I suppose my Matilda has told you that I love tellin' stories. Well, Mr. Behr, I have a story I'd like to tell ye."

It sounded more like a command than an invitation, and Everett bristled slightly. He doubted telling Mr. O'Dell that he didn't have time for stories would win him any points from the man. He dragged his desk chair from the inner office and offered O'Dell the seat. Tillie's father tossed his hat on the work counter and sat.

"A long time ago, a wee lass was born to a wretched man and his dear wife. The rogue wasn't worthy of such a sweet, beautiful baby girl child, but God saw fit to bless him anyways. One day, God took hold of this scurvy rascal and shook him so that he could finally see what a heathen he was. He told God he wanted to change his despicable ways and not hurt those he loved anymore, and God changed him. From that day on, that sweet little girl became the pride and joy of the man's life." O'Dell paused for a moment to clear his throat.

Tillie had already told him about her father's past, so it wasn't hard to figure out O'Dell was talking about himself. But why did the man think it necessary to tell Everett?

O'Dell placed both hands on his knees and continued his story. "One day, this man—*whist*—he turned around, and his baby girl was grown. 'When did this happen?' says he. Ah, but the man knows because he's watched his girl growin' into a beautiful young woman."

Tillie's father didn't have to remind him what a beautiful young woman she was. He spent his days and most of his nights trying to forget that very fact.

Mr. O'Dell held his chin between his thumb and forefinger and looked off to the side as though Tillie were standing there. "He's watched her so closely, mind you, that he knows every little thing about her—her laughin' and her cares, her wishin' and her hopin'. And the man knows when she's glowin' inside with joy and when her heart is breakin'— even though, the girl, she tries so hard to hide her woeful face from her da. She takes long walks all alone so she can do her cryin' in secret. But her da knows." O'Dell leaned forward and narrowed his eyes at Everett. "And this da wants to know what you did to make his baby girl cry."

The man could not have inflicted more pain if he'd run Everett through with a blade. He dipped his head and closed his eyes for a moment, trying to erase the picture O'Dell's story had painted in his mind.

"Mr. O'Dell, I hope you can believe me when I tell you it was never my intention to hurt Tillie. On the contrary, I was trying to spare her." He shook his head and raised his hand to run his fingertips over his scars. How could he tell this man who bore scars himself the real reason why he decided to stop seeing his daughter? "Mr. O'Dell. . .I couldn't. . .Tillie deserves better than me."

O'Dell's eyebrows arched. "Does she now? She told you that, did she?"

"Well, no, she would never. . . That's why I knew it was up to me. She's too tenderhearted." He stared down at his shoes, his stomach twisting into a knot. "Doesn't it bother you when people stare or when you see pity or repulsion in their eyes?"

"Are ye tryin' to tell me my Matilda pities you?"

Everett jerked his head up to meet Mr. O'Dell's steely gaze. "No! No, she doesn't. But other people do, and I couldn't ask Tillie to endure a lifetime of that. I'm sorry if that offends you, Mr. O'Dell, but I love your daughter too much to put her through that."

The moment the words blurted from his lips, Everett couldn't believe he'd spoken them. Fire rose up from his belly, searing his face almost as hot as the flames that had scarred him. He clamped his teeth together to prevent any more words from escaping.

Mr. O'Dell crossed one leg over the other. "So that's the way of it." The man angled his head and fixed his eyes on the trail the flames had made across Everett's face and neck. "Mm-hmm."

Everett fought to keep the grimace off his face under the man's scrutiny. It seemed O'Dell's eyes combed over every inch of his face.

Once his inspection was complete, O'Dell leaned back in the chair again. "I'm havin' a hard time understandin' exactly what 'tis you don't want to put my Matilda through."

Every reason, every argument Everett could employ would be an insult to the man sitting before him. His mind fought to put words into a coherent defense. "It's different for me than it was for you. You were already married and had children. You didn't have a choice. I do, and I choose to not hurt Tillie."

"It's a wee bit late for that way o' thinkin'. My Matilda is already hurtin'." Mr. O'Dell's expression softened. "Son, God won't never leave ye alone, in your joy nor in your troubles. That don't mean God will take your scars away, and I'm thinkin' the Almighty has a bit of work to do on you still. But don't be closin' the door on a blessin' He's tryin' to give ye."

Everett nodded mutely. He leaned his elbows on the work counter and rested his forehead in his hands. "A couple of weeks ago, I gave considerable thought to asking Tillie to the harvest picnic. I'd just about made up my mind, but. . ."

He could hear Mr. O'Dell shifting in the squeaky desk chair. "I'm put in mind of another story. There was these five frogs sittin' on a log. Four of 'em decided to jump off. So how many frogs was sittin' on the log?"

Everett had about had his fill of Irish stories, but respect dictated courtesy. "One?"

The man rose from the chair and clapped him on the back. "Why, there's still five frogs sittin' on the log. There's a difference between decidin' and doin'." O'Dell patted his shoulder. "Son, don't be runnin' from what God is tryin' to do in your life. The blessin's He gives us each day are the blessin's we need the most."

twelve

"Why did I even come here today?"

Even as he muttered the question to himself, Everett knew there were two answers, and neither of them had anything to do with satisfying his appetite. A makeshift table, constructed of wide planks the men had laid across several sawhorses, contained a scrumptious array of food that would tempt any normal man. From the safety of the shadowy cedars, Everett watched the women of the congregation load the tables to groaning, but the turmoil in his stomach left little room for food.

He'd finally given in to his father and Pearl and agreed to attend with them so they would stop pestering him. Understanding their good intentions soothed his irritation somewhat, but it wouldn't make the day any easier. Thankfully, they'd chosen a spot under the wide cedar boughs at the far edge of the churchyard, where he could distance himself from the activity.

The other reason was harder to define but no less compelling. It made no sense. Part of him wanted to see Tillie, even if it was from a distance. He wanted to see her smile, hear her laugh, and know she was enjoying herself. Satisfying himself that she was happy compelled him to scan the gathering of people, but the prospect of seeing her with Ben stirred his stomach into a whirlpool. Dread ate a hole in his heart.

From his vantage point, he found the pair making their selections at the food table, Ben's heaping plate dwarfing

Tillie's half-empty one. He escorted her to a blanket spread across the way, not far from the one where her parents sat. She wore her light green dress, the one that made her eyes look like pure green crystal, and something in his chest rolled over.

"This is the way it's supposed to be. She'll be happier with someone like Ben."

"Did you say something, son?" His father and Pearl returned to the blanket with quizzical expressions and three plates laden with all manner of delicacies.

"I was just talking to myself." He started to scoot farther back under the low-hanging cedar boughs, but Pearl passed a filled plate to him.

She gave him a motherly smile. "I hope you don't mind me bringing you a plate. I was afraid if I didn't, you wouldn't eat."

His father's wife was developing an uncanny insight into his thoughts and feelings, but he didn't resent it. Instead he found it comforting that she cared. He reached out to accept the plate and smiled his thanks to Pearl.

He took a few bites, forcing himself to swallow. The ladies of the church always brought their best culinary efforts to these affairs, but at the moment everything he put into his mouth tasted like sawdust. Only vaguely aware of the conversation between his father and Pearl, Everett kept his eyes trained on Tillie and Ben. Tillie smiled and nodded from time to time. Ben seemed to be doing most of the talking. Was it his imagination, or was Tillie looking out over the crowd of folks? Was she looking for him? He shifted his position, precariously balancing his plate, until he felt certain the shadow of the cedar boughs concealed him.

"How's business, son?"

Everett pulled his attention back to his father and stepmother. "Fine. We're staying busy." He managed a stiff smile and bit into a piece of fried chicken.

Pearl poured water from an earthenware jug into a tin cup and held it out to him. "Have you thought any more about the letter from the attorney?"

Everett nodded his thanks and accepted the cup. "I've done a lot of thinking."

Pearl's gaze lifted across the churchyard. Everett followed her line of sight, and his eyes landed on Tillie and Ben. What were they saying to each other? Tillie reached up and tucked a tendril of hair behind her ear, and angst lurched in Everett's stomach. He looked down at the drumstick in his hand, unsure of what he might do if Ben reached over to touch those honeyed strands.

Stop it. It's out of your hands. Let her go. Had he stayed long enough to appease his father and stepmother? If he got up to leave now, would people stare?

"Everett?"

He looked up from the partially eaten chicken leg he was studying. His father's expression indicated Everett had missed something. "Yes?"

Everett read compassion in the elder Behr's eyes. He suspected Father understood the turmoil swirling in his middle.

"I noticed you had a visitor the other day."

"I did?"

"Timothy O'Dell?"

"Oh." The Irishman's story of Tillie going off by herself to cry seared him again. "Yes, he stopped by."

When Everett didn't say more, and the silence was broken only by the hum of nearby voices and the laughter of playing children, Pearl rose from the blanket. "I think I'll go and cut some pieces of gingerbread cake for us."

Father gave her a soft smile and a nod, and another ache twisted in Everett's chest at the unspoken communication shared between their two hearts. There were times during his twilight walks with Tillie that even though the encroaching darkness prevented him from seeing her face clearly, he knew what she was thinking by the way she tipped her head or twirled a wildflower between her thumb and forefinger, or even by the way she stepped. What he had with her was something so special he couldn't put a name to it, and he was relinquishing it—just opening his hand and allowing it to fly away like a butterfly discovering it had wings.

His father cleared his throat. "This is none of my business, and you have every right to tell me to mind my own affairs, but I have a feeling Timothy didn't come calling with shipping freight in mind." The look he gave Everett was one of speculation.

"No." Everett blew out a pent-up breath through pursed lips. "He didn't." With one finger he traced the edge of the scar along his face. "He wanted to know what I did to make his daughter cry."

"Ah." His father lifted his bushy eyebrows but didn't ask his son to elaborate.

"Father, you must understand, I'm doing this *for* Tillie. She deserves someone better than me." He leaned back on his elbows and closed his eyes. "I'm not the one for her."

A snort came from his father's direction. "How did you come to that conclusion?"

He willed himself not to shoot back an angry retort. Taking in a calming breath, he pushed himself upright again. "Father, I will not subject Tillie to the humiliation of being seen with me. Why do you think we met and walked together in the evening? Nobody is standing around gawking at that time of night. What would people think if they saw her with me?"

Father stroked his mustache with his finger and shook

his head. "I must say, son, I never thought I'd hear you insult Tillie like that."

Everett jerked forward. "Insult her? What are you talking about? I'd never insult Tillie."

His father shrugged. "That's what it sounded like to me. You're certainly not giving her much credit. Tillie O'Dell isn't a shallow person, nor is she hypocritical. If she extended friendship and affection to you, you can rest assured it came from her heart. Don't you think you owe it to her to let her make up her own mind on the matter?"

Everett started to shake his head at his father's statement, but at that moment a commotion arose across the yard. He craned his neck to see around the cedar boughs. Tessa and Gideon Maxwell ran from one family's blanket to the next, calling their daughter's name.

"Susan! *Susan!*"

Several others joined the worried parents in searching around the immediate area and asking their children if they'd seen the little girl. They looked under the food table and the dessert table, and one of the women went to check the outhouse. Within a few minutes, every person was on their feet looking over the churchyard, calling the child's name.

Everett stood, his gaze fixed on Tillie as she crossed the yard to her friend. She took Tessa in her arms and held her tight, murmuring something into Tessa's ear. Tessa nodded and closed her eyes, her chest rising and falling with a deep breath.

Putting his abhorrence of being seen in public aside, Everett strode over to Gideon, who gathered Tessa in his arms. Tillie looked up as Everett approached. He locked eyes with her for a moment before turning to Gideon and waving Pastor Witherspoon over.

"Pastor, can you gather everyone together?"

The preacher nodded and hastily climbed the church steps and clanged the church bell. Everett grabbed Gideon's arm.

"She can't have gone far. We'll find her." He took the church steps two at a time to stand beside the preacher on the top step. Hiding his face didn't seem important with a child in danger.

"Folks, let's pair up and go in different directions. Some of you search in and around the church building. Others go over the yard again, and don't forget to check around the back. Still others spread out a little. A couple of teams should go down toward the creek. Don't leave a square foot unsearched. Pull back any low-hanging branches, and look in the bushes and underbrush. She might think she's playing hide-and-seek. Since she's so small—she's only. . .three?"—he looked to Gideon for confirmation—"she can fit into places we can't. When Susan is found, the church bell will be rung."

❧

As people teamed up and set off in specific directions, Tillie gave Tessa another hug. "We'll find her. You need to stay right here, because the first person she's going to want is you. Whoever finds her will bring her here."

Indecision tore through Tessa's eyes. Tillie knew she wanted to be out searching for her daughter but also saw the wisdom of the admonition. Tessa nodded, tears slipping down her face.

Tillie poured her friend a cup of coffee and guided her to the church steps to sit. She looked over her shoulder for Ben and found him approaching.

She gave him a timorous smile. "Why don't we look over by the mill."

Ben reached out and took Tillie's hand. "Why don't you and Everett pair up and look around the mill? I'll go check the brush behind the church."

Tillie blinked in surprise, and Ben released a small chuckle. "It's all right, Tillie. I can see in the way you look at him there's something special there. I'd sure like it if you looked at me that way, but I don't reckon that will happen as long as Everett is around." He squeezed her hand before releasing it. "You won't find a finer man than Everett Behr."

Hearing such praise coming from Everett's employee made her heart skip. "I hope I didn't—"

"You didn't. I knew all along he had your heart in his pocket."

Yes, he did, but what did it matter now? Everett had made it clear he had no intention of continuing their friendship. She gave Ben a parting smile and set off toward the mill. *"Why don't you and Everett pair up?"* She sighed and set her mind to finding little Susan.

Paying particular attention to the thick reeds and cattails along the side of the mill, Tillie pulled back every bit of growth at the edge of the stream that fed the mill's waterwheel. Susan's name echoed through the trees as the other searchers covered the area.

"Please, Lord, help us find her. Set your angels around her, keep her safe, and lead one of us to her."

"Amen."

Startled, she turned abruptly to find Everett behind her. Her breath caught in her throat, and she bit down on her lip. Everett had already distanced himself from her because she hadn't controlled her tongue.

"I've been saying the same prayer." He glanced over his shoulder at the teams of other folks looking for the child. "If she isn't found in a little while, we'll have to organize a more widespread search."

Tillie nodded mutely. She didn't want to think about the possibility of Susan not being found. She couldn't imagine the distress poor Tessa was experiencing.

She stood there, silently gazing at Everett, wanting her feet to move and return to searching, but unable to force them into motion. Finally, she found her voice, even if it did come out as a whisper. "Thank you for helping."

He lifted one shoulder and gave a slight nod, his lips pressed together. "Look, maybe you should go and stay with Tessa," he said, gesturing toward the church. "Gideon is out looking, and I think Tessa's by herself. She might need a friend."

Tillie's heart agonized, as much for Everett as for Tessa. "We all need a friend, Everett." She fixed her eyes on his face, and he didn't turn away. Did he understand the depth of her statement? Could she communicate with a look what she longed to tell him?

He held out his hand, and she transferred her gaze from his face to his fingertips. She slowly lifted her hand and placed it in his. The magic of his touch sent shivers through her.

He closed his hand around hers and steadied her as she stepped up the short embankment. When her feet were on level ground again, he dropped her hand, and she felt a pang of loneliness. She held back the sigh that wanted to escape.

"I haven't checked the other side of the mill yet."

Everett nodded. "I'll look there. Are you going to stay with Tessa?"

She glanced in the direction of the church and shook her head. "Miss Pearl is keeping Tessa busy while the rest of us search, so she's not alone." She started toward the little footbridge that led to the opposite bank of the stream and the stairs to the mill house. "I'm going to keep searching."

Everett fell into step beside her, turning his head from side to side, leaning down to part the cattails. "Do you know what

Susan was doing before Tessa discovered she was missing?"

Tillie stopped. "Tessa said she'd laid Susan down on their blanket for a nap and thought she was asleep."

A puzzled look crossed his face. "She could sleep with all the talking and laughing, and with the other kids playing and shouting?"

Tillie smiled at his lack of knowledge of children. "Most little ones can sleep through just about anything if they're tired enough." She sobered. "Tessa would never leave her alone if she thought Susan might wander off. She said she had only stepped away from their blanket for a few minutes to speak with Mrs. Witherspoon. When she went back to check on Susan, she was gone."

Everett's brows lowered into a frown. "Come on. Let's keep looking." He climbed the mill house stairs while Tillie covered every foot of space under the stairs and behind the mill.

"Susan!" *Oh Lord, please help us. Where is that child?*

☙

Despite the crisp autumn day, sweat collected on Tillie's forehead and trickled down her back after an hour of searching every conceivable place within a few hundred yards of the church. Her throat was growing hoarse from calling Susan's name.

The church bell clanged twice, and her heart leapt. *Oh praise God, she's been found!*

She picked up her skirts and ran but stopped short in the churchyard when she caught sight of a distraught Tessa standing by the steps with her arms wrapped around herself. Pastor Witherspoon motioned with his hand and called out for everyone to gather round.

"Folks, here's what we're going to do. The women will continue searching here in town, and the men are going to spread out and cover the hills and the woods. When Susan is found, either ring the church bell, or you men fire three shots. Let's step over to the table here and map out where all you fellows will go."

The women had cleaned off a section of the food table, and the makeshift structure now held a large coffeepot, cups, and the picnic leftovers, as if preparations for a long ordeal were being made. The ominous implication made Tillie shudder.

Pastor Witherspoon climbed down the stairs and paused just long enough to place a comforting hand on Tessa's shoulder.

Tillie hurried over to Tessa. She slipped her arms around her friend and held her without speaking. Tessa's shoulders began to shake.

"Oh, Tillie, where could she be?" Tessa broke into sobs. "I just want my little girl back. We were going to take her out to the Hamiltons' ranch tomorrow so she could pick out a lamb. She's talked of nothing else for the past week." She squeezed her eyes shut.

Tillie remembered Susan chattering nonstop about the "baby wams." She gripped Tessa's shoulders. "Tessa, by this time tomorrow you're going to be watching Susan playing with her pet lamb."

Some of the men headed out toward their assigned area, and Tillie looked to see which direction Everett was taking. Instead of tramping toward the hills, he was standing only a few away, looking at her and Tessa.

At the sound of galloping hooves, Tillie looked past Everett to see a rider coming in and recognized him as one of the hands from a nearby ranch. The man pulled his lathered mount to a stop in a cloud of dust, and several of the men, including the man's boss, ran over to hear what he had to say.

The young man dismounted and walked up to his boss. "We was out lookin' for strays, and we saw some buzzards circling overhead, so I went to check on it. There was a fresh kill—a young heifer." The ranch hand pulled off his hat and dragged his sleeve across his forehead. "It was a wolf kill. Just thought you'd want to know."

"Wolves?" One of the men sounded as though he didn't believe the report. "Why, there ain't been any wolves sighted around here for more'n a decade."

The rider nodded his head vehemently. "It was wolves all right. No mistakin' those tracks."

thirteen

"Noo!" Tessa's mournful wail pierced the air. *"Susan. . ."*

Tillie wrapped her arms around her rib cage and swallowed back the nausea that rose in her throat. She watched helplessly as Gideon crushed his wife to his chest for a long moment before leading her out of earshot of all the talk of wolves. A cold chill ran through Tillie. An image of horror tried to manifest itself in her mind, and she slammed the door on it, refusing to allow such ghastly thoughts.

Several of the men listening to the rider's report expressed skepticism. The young man's boss squinted at his employee. "You're sure it was wolves?"

The ranch hand nodded. "Yes, sir, I'm sure. The tracks resemble those of a dog, but about twice as big. Couldn't tell for certain, but I'm figurin' there were at least three or four, maybe more. You want to send some riders out to track them?"

The owner of the ranch scowled and told his employee about the missing child, instructing him to send the other hands out to search.

The murmur of voices around Tillie grew to a rumble as the level of urgency built. She tore her eyes away from the man who had delivered the grim news and turned around to look for Tessa and Gideon. They stood on the far side of the church, Tessa weeping against Gideon's shoulder. She hurried over and put her arm around Tessa, giving her shoulders a squeeze. Together, she and Tessa watched as Gideon strode to their wagon and pulled a rifle out from under the seat.

Old Cully stamped up the church steps and yanked on the bell rope. He cupped his hands around his mouth and hollered. "Some o' you men came to the picnic with your wagon and team. Iffen you need a saddle horse for searchin', come by the livery, and I'll loan you a mount. No charge."

"Matilda."

Tillie turned to find Da beside her. "I'm taking your ma and the younger ones home. Then I'm headin' out to search the area between our place and town. Phillip is partnerin' with Hubert Behr. Are you comin' home?"

Tillie gave Da a quick hug. "No, Da. I want to do what I can to help."

"How will ye be gettin' home?"

Tillie glanced from left to right and took her da's arm, stepping away from Tessa for a moment. "I'm sure I can find a ride from someone, but I might stay in town with the Witherspoons. I want to be close by, in case. . ."

Da patted her shoulder. "All right, daughter." He strode off, calling to her younger siblings to get in the wagon.

Ben Kiefer joined with Fletcher Hamilton, the owner of the sheep ranch, and headed south of the creek. A few of the other men paired up, and others set out alone, but all shared a common goal.

Gideon returned, rifle in hand. Tillie stepped back while he embraced Tessa. "We're going to find her. Hold on to that thought."

Tillie cast her gaze across the churchyard, squinting in the afternoon sun, seeking Everett. She located him standing by her family's wagon, talking with Da. Everett gestured to the northwest, and Da pointed toward the woods and then swept his hand in a southwesterly direction. Da gave Everett a nod and clapped him on the back before climbing into the wagon to drive his family home.

When Everett turned and his eyes met hers, she saw a tapestry of fear, compassion, and raw determination. A fleeting instinct told her his expression reflected the same emotions he'd felt before he entered the burning boardinghouse. He appeared to have forgotten about hiding his face.

She watched as Everett sent a pointed stare at Tessa, who wept in her husband's arms, as though he was trying to set in his mind the picture of this heart-sore mother. Gideon kissed his wife and set off at a run toward the livery.

Tillie closed the distance between her and Everett. He met her halfway and snagged her hand. "It's good she has a friend like you by her side while she waits for word. Keep telling her that we won't quit until we find her daughter."

Tillie drew her forehead into pinched furrows. When Everett released her hand, she caught his sleeve. "I'm going with you."

His eyes widened, and then a scowl darkened his expression. He grabbed her shoulders and gave her a little shake. "Oh no, you're not."

She opened her mouth to protest, but he laid his finger over her lips. His voice strengthened, and it was clear he would brook no argument. "You absolutely will not go out there. You will stay here—do you hear me?"

She'd never before witnessed in Everett the fervor she now saw in him. She stiffened her jaw and pressed her lips into a tight line. "Now you listen to me. Tessa is my best friend. I owe it to her to do everything I can to help find Susan. Standing around here twiddling my thumbs isn't going to find that little girl."

A flicker of something foreign flashed through Everett's eyes. It didn't stay there long enough for her to put a name on it, but if she had to guess, she'd have to call it a glimmer of panic.

He dropped his hands from her shoulders and took a step backward. Running his hand through his hair, he nailed her in place with his unblinking stare. He lowered the volume of his voice but not the resolute intensity. "Tillie, I don't have time to explain all the reasons it's so important that you remain here. But please listen to me. I need to be 100 percent focused on finding Susan, not worrying about your safety. I can't force you to stay, but I am imploring you. Please, Tillie." His voice cracked. "Please stay here so I'll know you're safe."

It was the first time he'd ever asked anything of her. All the times they'd walked in the shadow of the willows, not once had he stepped beyond the refuge of the defensive wall he'd erected. She'd gotten the impression he felt that allowing vulnerability was unthinkable. Yet here he stood, pleading with her to comply with his request. Held captive by the heartfelt ring in his voice and the depth of his mahogany eyes, Tillie tried to remember how to draw a breath. She gave him a slight nod.

His chest fell with a relieved sigh, and his voice took on a gentler pitch. "Take care of Tessa. Maybe you and a couple of the other ladies could put some of the picnic leftovers together for the men if they return hungry. We'll need lots of coffee." He glanced toward the west. "There's probably about three hours of daylight left. If we don't find Susan by sunset, we're going to need lanterns." He caught her hand and gave it a squeeze. "And I need you to pray."

Tillie nodded numbly. The ache in her heart for Tessa and Gideon, and the foreboding she felt over Susan's disappearance, paled for an instant. Making sure Everett knew he could depend on her became primary in her mind.

"I will—you can be sure of that."

A shadow of a smile relaxed some of the hard lines of

Everett's face. "Thank you." He scanned the wooded hills to the north and west. "She's such a little girl. It doesn't seem possible she could have gone farther than we've already looked." He returned his gaze to Tillie. "You don't suppose she's hiding, do you? Might she think this is a game, like hide-and-seek?"

Tillie's chest tightened, and she shook her head. "She can sometimes be a stubborn little thing, but she wouldn't hide for this long."

Everett blew out a hard breath. "Ring the bell if there's any news." He pulled his shoulders straight and tugged on the brim of his hat. He sent her a look she dared not interpret and headed into the woods.

Tillie followed him with her eyes until the sun-dappled autumn foliage swallowed him. She longed to be beside him, tramping through the woods, partnering with him. But this was no leisurely stroll. The mission before him, before all the searchers, could end in either joy or sorrow.

"Please, dear Lord, protect Susan wherever she is, and lead one of the men to her." She wiped away a tear. "And keep Everett from harm, Lord. Bring him back—" She started to ask God to bring him safely back to her, but reality insisted that he wasn't hers. Biting back the words wouldn't fool God. Her heavenly Father already knew her heart. "I love him, Lord. Please keep him safe."

≈

Everett paused beside the same small stream he'd found last Sunday morning when he'd hiked through the wooded hills. Scooping a few handfuls of water to his lips, he relished the coldness as the moisture soothed his throat. He cast another glance at the position of the sun and whispered a prayer that they'd find the child soon.

Instead of following the stream, he pushed deeper into the

woods. The underbrush was thicker than he'd anticipated, slowing his progress. Every fifty yards or so, he called out Susan's name and paused briefly to listen.

"It's simply not possible for a child of her age to have come this far." Or was it? What if she was following something, like a dog or a butterfly? How far would she go before she couldn't find her way back to the church? His limited knowledge of small children and their tendencies was a hindrance, but not if he trusted God to direct his steps.

"Lead me, Lord. Where is she?" A recollection prodded him. Hadn't he prayed a similar prayer as he crawled through the burning boardinghouse trying to find his father and Pearl? God had answered that prayer. Surely He'd answer this one.

Cupping his hands around his mouth, he called again, "Susan."

He plodded on, continuing to call her name and praying he would hear either the church bell echoing in the distance or three gunshots. The only sound accompanying him on his trek was the breeze rustling the leaves. If he found the little girl, he'd not be able to alert the others. He didn't own a gun, and looking for one to borrow would have taken precious time he didn't want to waste. Now he questioned the wisdom of hiking through the woods unarmed with the report of wolves in the area, but it was too late to turn back now.

Thorny brush snagged his pant legs and tore a hole in his sleeve as he pushed through a thick patch of blackberry canes. No berries remained on the vines this late in the season, reminding Everett that little Susan would likely be hungry and thirsty by now. But he guessed the first thing she'd want would be her mama.

"That's it!" He thrust out one hand, palm upturned. "I have to try to think like a three-year-old. What would she be looking for? She had to have a reason for wandering off."

He leaned against a birch tree and rested for a minute, rolling the questions over in his mind. What would be so fascinating to a three-year-old that it could entice her to leave her mother?

Daylight was slipping away. Through the trees he could see a slice of the sun sinking lower toward the western hills. This was the time of day he'd watched out the office window, waiting for the sun to hide its face so he could venture out. He'd gotten good at estimating the amount of daylight that remained. How many evenings had he impatiently wished the sun would hurry and disappear? Now he wished he could pray like Joshua did in the Old Testament for the sun to stand still. The fiery yellow sphere continued its downward slide. Once the sun set, finding the child would be nearly impossible, humanly speaking. Everett rejected that idea. Nothing was impossible when God moved in His miraculous way.

"Susan!" He pushed away from the tree trunk and pressed on. "Help me, Lord. Lead me. I don't know if making the sun stand still is in Your plans, but Lord, we need a miracle to find that little girl."

A fat squirrel chattered at him from a cottonwood tree. Everett barely gave the creature a passing glance, but something seemed to tug at him. Just what, he couldn't be sure, but he changed course and followed his instinct. The squirrel continued to scold him, and he wondered if Susan might find a squirrel intriguing enough to be lured into the woods. Most children loved animals, didn't they?

Think like a three-year-old. A thought grabbed hold of him. When Tillie was comforting Tessa, the child's mother had said something about. . .

"Lambs. She wanted to go see the baby lambs." He turned a slow, full circle. What direction would the child go if she thought she could find the lambs? The three-year-old wouldn't know how to find the ranch, but that didn't mean she wouldn't try. She'd probably pick the easiest terrain—flat instead of hilly, grass instead of thick underbrush. If she'd been to the ranch before, would she remember if there were trees or grassy hills along the way? He altered directions toward the edge of the woods.

Just as he started forward again, a rifle shot, fired some distance away, echoed. Everett held his breath, waiting for the second and third shots. *Please, God.* No accompanying shots sounded. A single gunshot. Whoever had fired it was likely shooting *at* something.

"Susan!" His throat was nearly raw from yelling. "Lord, please show me what direction she took." He tramped through the brush and saplings another fifty yards, his eyes scanning from left to right and his ears inclined, listening for a child's voice.

Jagged, splintered wood stuck out of a stump from a fallen tree to his right. Something clinging to one of the spearlike shafts of broken bole caught his eye. At first he thought it to be a common yellow butterfly. But this butterfly was very still. He climbed over the trunk of the tree lying in the midst of the underbrush. When he got closer, he saw it wasn't a butterfly at all. It was a small bit of yellow cloth.

He grabbed the bit of material and examined it, and then he raised his eyes to sweep the area. "Susan! Susan, can you hear me?"

Was the child wearing a yellow dress today at the picnic? He had no idea and couldn't remember if anyone had mentioned how the little girl was dressed. Holding the scrap aloft, he entreated God once again.

"Lord, is this hers? Did she come this way?" He searched the area around the stump to see if he could find anything else to indicate Tessa and Gideon's daughter had passed by there.

The sun hovered at the horizon. It would soon be dusk—usually his favorite time of day. But not today. He whispered the name of Jesus to send off pangs of despair. Over the past several months, he'd taken to singing whatever hymn he could recall from the previous Sunday to carry him through many difficult days. He racked his brain, trying to retrieve a hymn from his memory. Only one came to mind.

"Just as I am without one plea." He lifted his raspy voice, hoping Susan might hear and respond to the song.

Clutching the yellow scrap in his fingers, he pushed forward. The words of the song arrested his conscious thought. God, in His graciousness, hadn't refused to accept him, even with his past arrogance, deceit, and selfishness. God faithfully cleansed him of sin. But once redeemed, he'd refused to accept his own appearance, convinced he'd never be fit for polite company, and no woman would ever want to spend her life with him. How offensive his attitude must be to God.

"Lord, I'm sorry. I think I understand now. When I came to You just the way I was, You rescued me from my sinful self. But ever since then, I've hated my own reflection. You took me as I am. Now I choose to take me. . .just as I am." Instead of leaving a bitter taste, the notion of accepting himself, scars and all, was sweetly liberating. He slowed his steps and raised his eyes and his hands heavenward.

"Thank You, Lord." Resentment drained from him like water from a sieve. "Thank You."

The last sliver of sun was gone, and all that remained were the fading rays. He came to a small clearing and stopped, slowly scanning for some other indication that Susan had been there. An area of grass was matted flat, perhaps where a deer had lain down. Or a child.

"Susan!"

He listened. Nothing.

A huge orange moon was already rising in the darkening sky. "God, I won't be discouraged. You haven't brought me this far to abandon me. I trust You, Lord."

He judged direction by the waning light from the west. If he circled back toward town now, he could approach the church from a different angle and cover an area he'd not yet searched. Shadows deepened, and the air held a chill. Everett stopped to pull a thorny vine from his sleeve. A high-pitched wail carried on the shifting wind. Everett jerked his head up. Was it the cry of a child? He stood motionless, waiting to hear it again, to determine from which direction it came. When the eerie sound reached his ears once more, a shudder filled his being. It was the howl of a wolf.

fourteen

Poison darts of helplessness pierced Tillie's heart as the pastor's wife coaxed Tessa to the parsonage to rest for a while. How she wished there was something more she could do. Not having a child of her own, she could only imagine the searing ache attacking Tessa's heart. Determined to stay busy, she headed toward the long plank table, whispering repeated prayers for strength and courage.

Several ladies remained at the church while their husbands were out searching. Tillie joined them, offering sandwiches and coffee to the men who returned empty-handed but in need of a fresh horse. Regret pinched her. If only she hadn't promised Everett she'd stay put at the church. She knew this countryside far better than Everett did. Standing around handing out cups of coffee felt so. . . "Useless."

Pearl Behr slipped over and touched Tillie's shoulder. "Before Hubert left to go searching, he gave me the key to the mercantile and told me to take anything out of the storeroom that was needed. Would you mind coming along and helping me carry some lanterns and coal oil?"

Pearl's request sent an involuntary shiver down her spine as she glanced toward the west. The sun's fading rays set the sky afire with red and purple. The men would need lanterns soon. How she wished to hear three shots echoing across the hills. Nausea tightened her throat, but she nodded. "Of course."

Pearl patted her shoulder, and the two of them hurried off toward the mercantile. Tillie peered at Pearl's profile as they walked. "Tessa told me that you've been like a second mother to her."

The woman gave Tillie a tiny smile. "I suppose." Her voice sounded tight. "Little Susan is like the grandchild I never had." The distress that grew hour by hour showed in the deepened lines on Pearl's face, and Tillie's heart longed to offer comfort, but the words wouldn't form in the right order.

"I heard Cully say he was going to make some torches to put around the churchyard in case. . ." She bit back the words she didn't want to speak.

As they stepped up onto the boardwalk in front of the store, Tillie noted the lengthening shadows and the dipping temperature. Another whispered entreaty—part of her continuous prayer—winged toward the throne of heaven. While she appreciated Cully's thoughtfulness in supplying the torches, she prayed Susan would be found before darkness set in, and neither the torches nor the lanterns would be necessary.

Pearl slid the key into the lock and pushed the door open. "Hubert and your brother Phillip went east. He said they planned to go as far as Rock Creek and zigzag back through the hills."

Tillie frowned. "Rock Creek is almost two miles from here. Susan never could have gotten that far. She has to be somewhere close, somewhere we haven't looked." They paused for a moment to look at each other. "But where haven't we already looked?"

Pearl began pulling lanterns off the storeroom shelf and handing them to Tillie. "Some of the ladies got tired of waiting and went to retrace their steps over many of the places around town that have already been searched. Maybe someone will find her curled up asleep."

They each took as many lanterns as they could carry, along

with a can of coal oil, and made their way back to the church. No rifle shots or the church bell ringing had called to them while on their errand. They arranged the lanterns on the plank table opposite the coffeepots.

Since Tessa was in Mrs. Witherspoon's capable hands, Tillie felt free to slip into the church for a solitary moment of prayer. Muted noises and voices from the churchyard followed her, but none carried the joyful excitement of good news.

The hours since Everett left had crawled by. She tried to fill the time, keeping her hands occupied with helpful tasks, but more important than brewing pots of coffee or making sandwiches was keeping her promise to Everett. The only thing he'd requested, other than for her to remain at the church, was for prayer, and she set her heart to honor his request. Intercession for Everett's protection and Susan's safe return flowed between her lips and heaven. The imploring tone of his voice and the memory of his face when he'd insisted she stay behind where she'd be safe brushed her senses. So much of their time together over the past months she'd spent looking at only his profile in the shadows—she'd never had the opportunity to look into the depth of his eyes. Most of the time he'd kept his heart as guarded as his countenance, but there were a few moments that had revealed brief glimpses into the things that molded Everett's character. Only on rare occasions had Everett shared anything of a more personal nature. Vulnerability wasn't something he allowed, and to finally see uncloaked emotion on his face had left her breathless.

She sank to her knees and leaned her elbows on a pew, holding her head in her hands. The moment she closed her eyes, images of Everett and Susan—and wolves—emerged in her mind.

"He's doing the same thing he did the day he ran into the burning boardinghouse, Lord. He's hidden his face for a year, and what drew him out from behind his defensive stronghold was hearing a child was in danger. It's like he's running into a burning building again, except this time he's tramping around in the woods and hills unarmed, with wolves in the area." Tears burned her eyes, and she swiped at her nose with her sleeve. "He's not thinking of himself at all. Lord, please keep him safe. He didn't even take a gun."

Her chest tightened. "Lord, of course my heart is burdened for Susan's safety and Tessa's anguish. But as always, I'm lifting Everett up to You. Everything I have ever felt for this man is magnified.

"You've heard my prayers asking You to put Everett and me together. I even ran ahead of You and tried to make it happen using my own selfish devices, because I wasn't willing to wait for You to reveal Your plan to me. Lord, that was wrong. Please forgive my impatience and impulsiveness. There are no secrets from You. You already know I love Everett, and I ask You now, if my love for him isn't Your will, then please remove this love from my heart. And if Everett doesn't love me, please give me the grace to accept it."

Tears welled and spilled over. Uttering the words, even to God, impacted her with such force it nearly knocked the breath from her. Rushing headlong into her own plans had ended in disaster. Waiting for God's plan to unfold stretched her trust farther than she had believed possible.

"Dear God, my heart is in Your hands. You are everything I need. The longing of my heart is for Everett and me to be together, but even more than that I want to be obedient to You." She took a deep breath and swallowed hard. "You are my rock, Lord Jesus."

She dug in her pocket for her handkerchief and dabbed

at her eyes and blew her nose. "Please be with Everett as he searches. Be with all the men, watch over them, and please, dear Lord, please let one of them find Susan soon. Prayer is the most important thing I can do. I'm sorry for feeling so impatient, wanting to do more."

Tillie continued in prayer, begging God for His mercy and protection for Susan, comfort for Tessa, and strength for the men searching. She opened her eyes and raised her head off the pew at which she was kneeling. The air had turned chilly, and the fading light that had accompanied her into the church was gone. She pushed away from the pew and rose from her knees. There were lanterns to fill.

꘎

Everett tipped his head up and watched with appreciation as the moon slowly rose higher in the inky sky, gradually changing from orange to gold to bright white as it ascended. He couldn't remember ever seeing such a large, bright moon, bathing the countryside in silver. Tillie's father had said something about a harvest moon. Everett didn't know the difference between a regular moon and a harvest moon, but as he gazed across the illuminated landscape, he whispered his gratefulness to God for supplying just what he needed to pick his way through the darkness.

The underbrush gave way to meadow grass as he emerged from the woods. He hoped he would come across another stream or spring. Why hadn't he thought to bring a canteen with him? His throat was parched with thirst and raw from yelling Susan's name.

"If I'd used common sense, I'd have taken a few minutes to borrow a canteen and a gun." He shook his head at his foolish impulsiveness.

His feet throbbed and legs ached from hours of hiking, and weariness dogged him. Oh, how he'd love to lie down in the grass and indulge in blessed sleep. But the memory of the wolf howl he'd heard earlier continued to send chilling echoes through his mind. He pushed on.

A few clouds drifted lazily, occasionally obscuring the pale light. Everett paused, waiting for the spooky veil that slowed his progress to move away from the moon. Maybe he should take a few minutes to rest. No, the picture he'd burned into his mind of Susan's distraught mother wouldn't let him stop.

A few trees dotted the meadow, and many of them had shed much of their foliage. Drizzled with mottled moonlight, the branches created curious patterns overhead. The temperature had dropped rapidly once the sun disappeared, and the scent of frost piqued his awareness. It was unlikely Susan wore a coat, and he imagined the little tyke shivering in the cold.

Quiescence reigned over the landscape. Only an occasional breeze rattled the remaining leaves, but even the slight wafting made the air feel colder. At least when there was no wind, he could hear more clearly.

A rustling sound stopped him in his tracks. He turned his head in the direction from which he thought the noise had come, only to hear it again, this time coming from near the woods. The clouds chose that moment to draw their shroud over the moon, plunging him into near blackness. His heart pounded in his ears, and despite the chill in the air, beads of sweat popped out on his upper lip. He tried to hold his breath, but his lungs betrayed him by sucking in a raspy hiss.

Another crackling sound behind him, like stepping on fallen leaves, sent a shudder through him. It might simply be a raccoon or opossum. How did one tell the difference between the sounds made by a foraging animal and a stalking animal? He held his breath and listened hard, praying he wouldn't hear growling. It was impossible to calculate the size or weight of the animal by the rustle of grasses and leaves. The sound seemed to come from more than one direction. Was his mind playing tricks on him, or did the stillness of the cold night air alter the sound? There it was again, this time to his left.

What if it was Susan? Should he call out to her?

What if it isn't Susan? A drop of sweat ran down his neck into the collar of his shirt.

A slight breeze stirred, and an owl hooted from a nearby tree. An explosion of noise erupted from the grass. His heart seized with a jolt, and he instinctively threw his arms up in front of his face. Two or three animals bounded into the woods, the sound of their feet leaping through the brush growing fainter as they retreated. Deer, most likely. Everett's knees wobbled, and his stomach twisted with nausea. The breath he struggled to control moments earlier now came in great gulps. He bent at the waist and propped his hands on his knees.

"Thank You, God."

He waited until his pulse returned to almost normal and the moonlight once again befriended him before he straightened. The owl hooted again, and Everett squinted up through the tree branches. "I suppose you're amused by that." He sent an accusing glare into the trees limbs, and the owl replied with a series of doleful *whoo-whoos*.

The sound reminded Everett of the prayer he'd prayed a few weeks ago for God to make something beautiful of his life. *Something beautiful, beautiful. . .*

He pressed on through the meadow, moonlight and clouds creating a strange patchwork of silver and shadow. The owl's hoots followed him, floating on the still night air. Instead of sounding like a taunt, it fell on his ears in a soothing reminder of God's hand liberating him from his self-made prison.

Everett smiled. "Lord, I don't know what direction You will take me or how You plan to work in my life. I only know the best place, the safest place, for me to be is within Your hand. If I stay there, I believe You *will* make something beautiful happen. Guide me, Lord, through this night. Whatever path You've charted for me, keep me close to You."

Something beautiful. Something beautiful. Heaven spilled affirmation over him, as if God was agreeing with his prayer. Weariness drained away. A fresh spurt of energy flowed. Uplifted, Everett called out again. "Susan. Susan."

What was that? An unidentifiable sound reached him. Another animal? He stopped, all of his senses piqued. The breeze picked up again and stirred the leaves and grass.

There it was again. A frail squeak filtered through the soft whooshing of the wind. Did Gray follow him out here? Silly cat.

He was about to move on when the muted mewing sound penetrated the darkness once more. "Gray? Is that you?"

When no meow replied, he shook his head, chagrined. Perhaps his imagination was getting carried away. He ran a hand through his hair. How long had he been out here? Four hours? Longer? With the light of the moon, he moved on in what he hoped was the direction of the church. His foot stumbled on a low spot, and he realized he'd come across a tiny rivulet, no doubt coming from a spring somewhere higher. Grateful, he bent on one knee to quench his thirst. As he was sucking in the third handful of water, the squeaky cry reached him again, but this time it was closer. And it spoke.

"Mama."

The water slipped through his fingers, and he jerked his head up. "Susan?" He pushed to his feet. "Susan?"

He heard a tiny sob and hiccup. "Mama."

Joy stirred in his middle and rose up, much like the joy he'd felt last year after the fire when he'd learned his father and

Pearl were safe. "Susan, where are you? Keep calling so I can find you."

Another weak cry rode on the breeze to his ears. "Mama."

"I'm coming, Susan. I'm coming."

"Mama." Her voice grew stronger.

As the air currents moved the clouds away from the moon, a shaft of radiance like a beam from heaven widened across the meadow and revealed a patch of pale yellow at the base of a tree. Everett headed toward it. "I'm coming, Susan."

"I want Mama."

A grin split Everett's face. He'd never heard such sweet words. A few more strides and he lowered himself to one knee in front of the little girl in the yellow dress. "Hey, do you know how many people are out looking for you?"

Susan tipped her face up and stared at him. She shook her head.

"Are you all right? Are you hurt anywhere?" He sent an anxious scan over her face and arms. No visible blood.

She held out one arm and twisted it around, pointing to a place near her elbow. "Ow."

Everett couldn't see much in the pale light, but based on Susan's description of her injury, it was minor. A wave of relief washed over him.

The little girl chattered her teeth. "I cold." She reached out her arms, and Everett gathered her close to his chest. She snuggled her head onto his shoulder.

He pulled his chin back and looked down at her. "I'll bet you want to go home, don't you?"

Moonlight shimmered off the tears on her plump cheeks. "I want Mama." She locked her arms around his neck.

"I know, honey." He patted her back. "Can I put you down for a minute?" He set her in front of him, and she leaned against his bended knee. A mixture of fatigue and exhilaration made his fingers fumble with the buttons on his shirt, but he pulled the garment off and wrapped it around her. It wasn't a blanket, but it was the best he could do. He tugged the collar higher around her neck and face, and then adjusted his suspenders over the shoulders of his long johns.

"Let's go back over here and get a drink of water. Then we'll go home."

He carried her back a few paces where the tiny stream cut through the meadow. Cupping his hand, he scooped up several handfuls of water for the little tyke, who slurped at the moisture noisily.

She leaned forward and peered up at his face. "Are you a angel?"

Everett chuckled and dabbed at her wet face with the tail of the shirt. "No, honey. My name is Everett, and I'm going to take you home."

"Ever." She wrapped her arms around his neck again.

He rose with the little girl safely snuggled in his arms. She felt like an aspen leaf quivering in the wind. Shivers rippled through her tiny, lithe body. Everett positioned his arms to cover as much of her as he could, hoping he could give her some of his warmth. Again he berated himself for not bringing a gun. The other searchers and those waiting at the church wouldn't know he'd found Susan until he arrived back at Willow Creek with her.

If he kept the woods to his left and followed them, he should eventually find the town. With a prayer of gratitude on his lips, he headed toward the church with as much speed as his limited vision and small burden would allow. The very thought of placing the little girl in her mother's arms filled him with unspeakable joy.

fifteen

Tillie's chest tightened at the sound of Tessa's soft weeping. Mrs. Witherspoon sat beside the distraught mother, holding Tessa's hand. Tillie rolled her head from side to side, working out the kinks in her neck and easing the tension in her shoulders. If only she could do the same for Tessa's heart.

Tillie poured three cups of coffee and served sandwiches to the trio of men who'd dragged in minutes earlier, reporting they'd seen no sign of the little girl. With apologetic glances in Tessa's direction, the men spoke quietly of the ground they'd covered and the thoroughness of their search. Tillie listened to their exchange with a sinking heart as they gulped down their food.

One of the men talked around the bite of sandwich in his mouth. "We heard that one rifle shot. Hoped it meant the little one had been found, but"—he shrugged—"there weren't but one shot, so we kept lookin'."

The other men nodded, and one of them jerked his thumb toward another pair of searchers. "Todd Finnigan said he took a shot at a wolf he saw in the distance, but the critter was out of range."

Tillie glanced toward Mr. Finnigan, who was filling a lantern with coal oil. Though discouraged over not having found Susan yet, none of the men who'd come back for a fresh horse or something to eat talked of giving up. For that, Tillie was grateful.

Tillie carried a canteen to the pump at the side of the building and worked the handle up and down, filling the vessel. She fastened the closure and crossed the yard to hand the canteen to Todd Finnigan.

"Mr. Finnigan, where was that wolf you saw?"

The dancing light from the torches seemed to deepen the worry lines in the man's face. "Southwest of here, across Devil's Backbone Hill, near the edge of the woods."

Tillie shook her head slightly. "Do you really think Susan could have wandered that far?"

He accepted the canteen and shrugged. "Who knows? I've seen little ones move faster than the parents thought they could." He slung the canteen onto his shoulder. "Personally, I hope she's found right here, holed up in some little out-of-the-way nook no one thought to check. I know you ladies are still looking all over town." He tugged the brim of his hat and picked up the lantern. "Thanks for the water and the grub."

The man stepped beyond the torchlight and disappeared into the darkness. With a sigh, Tillie poured another cup of coffee and picked up the old quilt she and Ben had sat upon hours earlier. So much had transpired—the picnic was a faded memory. She crossed the yard to the church steps and handed Tessa the cup. Tessa shook her head, but Tillie nudged it toward her insistently. "Drink it. You need something in your stomach." She unfolded the quilt and draped it around Tessa's trembling shoulders. "Mrs. Witherspoon, why don't you go get yourself something to eat. I'll stay with Tessa."

The pastor's wife smiled and rose, nodding toward the church door. "Some of the ladies have started a continuous prayer time inside. Two or three are in there praying right now. After a while some others will spell them."

Tillie nodded. "I'll join them in a bit." She sat down and slipped her arm around Tessa. "Did you get any sleep?"

Tessa shook her head. "No, but Mrs. Witherspoon made

me rest even if I couldn't sleep." She released a shaky sigh. "Oh, Tillie, what if—"

"Stop!" Tillie held up her hand. "Don't even think like that. There are dozens of men out there combing every inch of the woods and meadows and hills." She rubbed Tessa's back. "Mr. Finnigan said she's probably right around here somewhere in a place we haven't looked. She'll wake up hungry and start crying for you, and wonder what all the fuss is about."

Tessa nodded and took a swallow of coffee. "Has Everett come back yet?"

At the mention of his name, a rush of warmth filled Tillie's chest and traveled up her neck. She shook her head. "No, not yet. I'm sure he's just being thorough." She didn't voice the fear that had run through her head a dozen times already. *He's not as familiar with these hills as the other men. What if he got turned around and can't find his way back to the church?*

Tessa's soft voice broke into her thoughts. "I'm sure he'll come in anytime now."

Tillie blinked at her friend's insight and unselfish expression of comfort. "Of course he's fine. So is Susan. We're the ones who have the hardest job of all—waiting."

"Matilda."

Tillie glanced up to see her father trudging across the yard. "Da." She trotted over to greet him, clutching his arm the instant they met. There was no need to ask the question that burned in her heart. Da's weary eyes and discouraged countenance gave her all the answers she needed. "Da, come and sit down. I'll bring you some coffee and a sandwich."

" 'Twould be a blessin', for sure." He sat on the grass and leaned back on his elbows.

Tillie hurried to the table and assembled a sandwich from leftover chicken. Having a task to occupy her hands vented some of her nervous energy, but her mind and heart still yearned to see Everett emerge from the darkness. Immediately, her conscience was smitten. "Lord, it's selfish to think of my own feelings for Everett at a time like this." She glanced over her shoulder at Tessa, who remained on the church steps, looking forlorn with Tillie's quilt draped around her. "Lord, please surround little Susan with Your angels, and bring her back home to Tessa and Gideon." She put the sandwich on a tin plate. "Since You're already working in the midst of this crisis, I beg You, heavenly Father, to bring Everett back safely as well."

She took her father the food and coffee and sat next to him while he ate. He took a noisy slurp. "Ah, 'tis good coffee. It'll warm up me innards."

Tillie scanned the yard, taking in the handful of men, some of whom had just arrived and others who were preparing to go back out. Her gaze moved from left to right until it landed on Tessa. Every time she looked at her friend, Tillie's heart cramped. Da also glanced in Tessa's direction, a deep furrow in his brow.

"Poor girl." He shook his head.

"Da, do you have any idea what areas the men have covered?"

Da munched on his sandwich and chased it down with a swallow of coffee. "Hubert Behr said he and Phillip planned to cover the area from his house south and east. Jed Brewer said he and his boy would go straight east from town to the Clermont road and then circle back toward the north. I covered the stretch between here and our place. Then I headed west a ways and crossed back to that rocky place in the hills where you kids used to go and play." He took another bite. "Has Everett been back yet?"

Tillie shook her head. "When he left here, he was going toward the woods."

Da stuffed the last bite of sandwich into his mouth, chewing thoughtfully. "Mm. He planned to search through the woods. I told him a bit about the lay of the land, him bein' here only a year. Showed him on a sketch how the woods curve to the northwest and meet Devil's Backbone Hill. That's the area he was searchin'. You say he ain't been back in? He should have covered that area by now."

The blood in Tillie's veins froze, and a quiver shuddered through her that had nothing to do with the chill in the air. "Devil's Backbone?"

"Aye." Da hoisted himself to his feet.

Tillie scrambled to snatch Da's sleeve before he could take a step. "Da, Mr. Finnigan said he spotted a wolf near there. He took a shot at it, but it was too far away."

"Ah, that must've been the shot I heard." He slipped his arm around her. "Don't fret, daughter. Everett can take care of himself."

"But Da, he didn't take a gun with him."

Da halted his steps and turned to face her. "Why in heaven's name not?"

She lifted her shoulders. "I don't think he owns one, but that's not important now. Da, he's out there tramping around in the dark, unarmed, in an area where a wolf was sighted."

Da's lips thinned into a grim line, and he cast a hard squint toward the woods. "Fetch me a lantern, daughter. Is Finnigan still here?"

Tillie shook her head. "He left about fifteen minutes before you came in." She pointed in the direction the man headed when he left. "He went that way."

Her father blew out a stiff breath and crossed the yard where two other men with lanterns were preparing to head back out. Tillie scurried to the makeshift table to do her father's bidding. Her hands shook as she tilted the can to pour coal oil into the lantern reservoir, and she spilled some on the table. The acrid odor of the lantern fuel burned her nose, but it was the image in her mind of Everett encountering a wolf in the dark that brought tears to her eyes.

⊱

The image in Everett's mind of Tillie's wide green eyes the last time he saw her accompanied him as he tramped through the dark with little Susan in his arms. The moon continued to play hide-and-seek, at times casting the hillside in brightness, sometimes shedding just enough light for him to take a few steps, and sometimes slipping behind a cloud, encasing him in blackness.

He paused, waiting for the nocturnal light to make its appearance again. Susan whimpered against his shoulder and tightened her grip around his neck. He patted her back.

"It's all right. The moon is just playing a game with us. It will peek out again in a minute." To soothe the child, he started to sing.

"Rock of Ages, cleft for me; let me hide myself in Thee." The words spilled comfort over him, reminding him once again of the only hiding place he ever wanted to seek for the rest of his life. When he couldn't remember all the words to the hymn, he hummed the melody.

Susan raised her head off his shoulder. "Ever, where's my mama?"

Despite their precarious situation, Everett smiled. "She's probably at the church waiting for us, honey." He patted her again, and she laid her head back down.

He continued humming. A moment later the moon reemerged, spilling pocketfuls of pale radiance across the meadow. The trees at the edge of the woods had mostly lost their leaves, casting grotesque shadows like dancing skeletons.

Everett peeked down at Susan and was glad to see her head faced away from the spooky patterns.

"Rock of Ages, cleft for me; let me hide myself in Thee. Hmm-mm, hmm-mm."

The wind picked up again, raising gooseflesh on his arms and across the back of his neck. Everett couldn't be sure of the time. He hadn't bothered to wear his watch and chain when he dressed for the picnic, not that he could have dug it out of his pocket without disturbing Susan anyway. How long had it been since the sun had set? Two hours? Three? Curious how being far from town and enveloped in darkness skewed one's judgment of the passing of time. As chilled as he was, it felt like he'd been walking all night.

Using the edge of the woods as his guide, he pressed forward, praying he was heading in the right direction. What if he was headed away from town?

Please, Lord, lead me home.

Weariness made his feet feel like they were wading through a snowbank. His stomach growled, reminding him he'd not eaten for hours. How much longer had it been since Susan had eaten? His arms tightened around the little girl. She wasn't complaining. Of course, he guessed she was more tired than hungry. His own fatigue was beginning to toy with his sense of direction, not to mention his ability to think straight. Even the sounds of the night teased him into imagining things, like the eerie howl he thought he heard a moment ago. Nonsense. It was just the wind.

The rifle shot he'd heard—how long ago had that been?— seemed to echo through the woods. It was impossible to tell from which direction it had come. Was it the darkness or exhaustion that made him so disoriented?

He took a step, and the ground beneath his foot gave way. His ankle turned, shooting pain up his leg as his balance faltered. He stiffened his back to keep from falling. Steadying himself with his left foot, he pulled the right one free of the gaping burrow—probably a gopher hole. He gritted his teeth and took several deep breaths, waiting for the throbbing to recede. After a few minutes he tried putting weight on the injured foot. Sharp spasms wrapped around his ankle, but he managed to walk. His uneven gait jostled Susan, but she didn't protest.

His body cried out for rest. When he'd first gathered Susan into his arms and snuggled her onto his shoulder to keep her warm, she had been light as a feather. Now she felt like some of the crates he hauled on and off the freight wagon every day. How could one small girl weigh so much? His back ached, and the scars on his shoulder burned as they stretched under his precious burden.

Just put one foot in front of the other.

Susan stirred in his arms, and he peeked down at her. "Are you all right, Susan?"

No response.

"Susan?" He angled his head and tried to see if her eyes were closed, but judging by her limp form, she'd fallen asleep. Good. At least if she was asleep, she wouldn't be frightened. Hopefully, the next time she opened her eyes, he would be handing her to her mother.

The moon disappeared behind a cloud again, forcing him to stop. He needed to rest his ankle anyway. He tugged the collar of his shirt up a little higher around Susan's neck. While he waited for the cloud to ride across the sky and reveal the moon again, he tried to train his eyes to pierce through the darkness. A tiny pinpoint of light floated across his bleary vision. A firefly? He fixed his stare on the friendly insect.

"How nice of you to keep us company in the middle of

the night," he said. But not only did this firefly stay in one place; its glow also didn't fade. Everett frowned. Fireflies were plentiful in the warm months of summer, but in late September in the brisk autumn temperatures? The firefly still didn't move.

"That's not a firefly." His pulse picked up. Was he so drained of strength he was seeing things? He glanced at the sky and was rewarded with a glimpse of the moon's glow at the edge of the cloud. In a few moments he could proceed again.

A flash of panic struck him. He'd taken his eyes off the firefly—or whatever it was—to search for the moon. He jerked his eyes forward again. There it was. His breath deepened with a stirring of hope.

Thin moonlight once again splashed softly across the hillside. The pinpoint of light shone like a beacon through the edge of the woods. He set his course straight in its direction, like a ship toward a lighthouse. Periodically the firefly disappeared as he picked his way through the trees, but it always reappeared. Underbrush snagged his trouser legs and threatened to trip him, but he limped on.

Two fireflies now winked ahead of him. His heart accelerated. It had to be the town. His ankle ached with every step, and Susan still lay like deadweight on his shoulder, stretching the scarred tissue, but the discomfort no longer mattered. Fresh determination propelled him through the woods.

Two lights became three, peeking in and out of the brush. He became vaguely aware that he was panting. He stubbed his foot against something hard and unforgiving. A rock? Without shifting Susan, he extended his leg, poking the obstacle with his foot. A fallen tree.

Not wishing to lose sight of the lights, he slid his left leg over the tree trunk, but doing so meant putting all his weight on his painful right ankle. He clamped his teeth and bit back the groan that tried to escape. Lowering his torso to straddle the tree, he carefully swung the other leg over and rose. Susan remained slumped against him. As he stood, his eyes searched through the woods for the lights to anchor his position. Was it his imagination, or did he smell coffee?

His throbbing ankle begged him to stop, but the flickering lights drew him. They grew and danced between the trees. A soft glow outlined a rooftop and a steeple. He'd found the church. A joy-filled shout gathered deep within his chest, but his throat constricted, preventing the expression of exultation from escaping. It was just as well. He didn't want to frighten Susan. He limped past the edge of the woods and came to the feathery cedar trees that lined the churchyard—the same cedars he'd used as a hiding place countless times. With a prayer of thanksgiving on his lips, he stepped beyond the refuge of the cedars and into the torch and lantern light.

sixteen

Tillie tipped the can of coal oil to extract the last few drops into the reservoir of the lantern. Her brother Phillip stood a few paces away, blowing on a cup of coffee and taking tentative sips. All the men who'd straggled in throughout the evening looked just the way Phillip did, bedraggled and discouraged, hungry and tired.

"Can I get something to eat, Tillie? I'm starved."

If she hadn't felt so emotionally battered, she'd have grinned. Phillip was always starved.

"All the picnic leftovers are gone. The women made sandwiches until we ran out of ham, chicken, and bread." She set the coal oil can aside. "Mr. Kyle at the hotel said we could use the hotel kitchen to prepare food for everyone. As soon as I'm finished filling these lanterns—"

Her words were drowned out by a shout that rang through the still night air. In her distracted state, Tillie wasn't sure she'd heard the words correctly, but she could have sworn it sounded like the person was praising God. She looked up and saw several people running. Another shout, then another. A jolt shot through her.

"Mercy, what's happened?" She and Phillip both spun in the direction the folks were running. A jubilant chorus split the air. The sight that greeted her buckled her knees. When she opened her mouth, she couldn't push out a single syllable, but her lips formed one silent word. *Everett*.

She was afraid to blink. Indescribable joy welled up within her and could not be contained. Grateful tears and pure

157

laughter blended like a fine tapestry in her soul.

All the shouting awakened the sleeping child snuggled in Everett's arms, and, apparently startled, Susan shrank closer and clung to him as he crossed the yard to the church steps. Tessa rose, her expression a mixture of elation and solace, gratitude and relief. Tears poured down her face as she reached out to receive her child.

Tillie slipped her hand up to cover her mouth, holding in the sobs as Everett placed Susan in her mother's arms. Was that Everett's shirt wrapped around the tyke? Unchecked tears seeped through her fingers as she witnessed the reunion for which they'd so fervently prayed. Instead of doing what she longed to do—running and throwing her arms around Everett's neck—she stood nailed in place, watching others thump him on the back and pump his hand. Some of the ladies squeezed his arm, and Pearl stood on tiptoe and kissed his cheek.

Susan wiggled and pulled back from her mother's tight hug and pointed at Everett. "Look, Mama. God sended me a angel. His name is Ever."

Amid the chuckles, Tessa stepped over to Everett with grateful tears in her eyes. "How can I thank you? You gave me my little girl back. You *are* an angel." Susan, now cocooned in the old quilt that had earlier draped Tessa's shoulders, sent Everett a sleepy smile.

Someone leaped up the church steps and began pulling on the bell rope, sending peals of jubilation ringing through the town and surrounding hills and calling in the searchers. Each happy clang of the bell resounded with good news. Across the countryside, trios of rifle shots echoed in response, proclaiming to everyone within hearing radius that God had answered their prayers.

Pastor Witherspoon climbed the steps and called for everyone's attention. He led the gathering in a prayer of praise and thanksgiving for Susan's safe return. As soon as everyone whooped, "Amen!" he raised both hands.

"I think I speak for all of us when I express how grateful we are to Everett Behr, and to all the folks who helped search for little Susan. Everett, you're a bona fide hero." More "amens" rose among those gathered, along with shouts of affirmation.

Tillie couldn't take her eyes off Everett. Normally he ducked his head or covered his face and fled from the presence of a large group like this. But he was hemmed in by the townsfolk and couldn't escape even if he wanted to. The public praise brought a flush to his cheeks, but there was something else—something normally absent from his face: a smile. Her heart accelerated. Her hungry eyes took in every plane of his dear countenance.

Pastor Witherspoon continued, "I think you'll agree we're all too tired for a barn dance." A few murmurs and groans of concurrence resonated. "So if it's all right with everyone, and if it's all right with Dan Miller, whose barn we planned to use, we'll hold the harvest dance next Saturday night." More nods and hums of agreement rippled through the group.

A few pairs of searchers came galloping in, among them Gideon Maxwell, who leapt off his horse and ran to embrace his wife and daughter. Tillie wrapped her arms around herself to contain the happy shiver dancing in her chest, and enjoyed the scene as Gideon added his thanks to Everett.

The feelings that swelled her heart went far beyond admiration. Tillie's feet itched to run to Everett, and her fingers trembled in anticipation of touching his hand. Still she held back, waiting for people to disperse. What she wished to tell Everett was best said in quiet and privacy.

Tillie remained off to the side, her gaze locked on the man in the center of the gathering. If she could communicate silently across the space that separated them, she'd already spoken volumes. Finding the words to vocalize her thoughts and feelings to him, however, was a different matter. If only he could simply read her heart.

Everett turned his head from one side to the other. He appeared to be searching the crowd. At no time since he walked in with Susan in his arms had Tillie seen him attempt to hide his scars, and he wasn't doing so now. He craned his neck and turned around. The moment his gaze met hers, she felt the impact. A tiny smile hooked the corner of his mouth and stretched the scars on the right side of his face. Her heart thumped out a rhythm she was certain he could hear, even over the celebration taking place around them. Neither of them looked away. Did he know what she was thinking? Could he hear with his heart what her lips couldn't speak?

Gradually the people called out their final good nights to each other, patting Susan on the head and shaking Everett's hand. A few of the ladies began packing the last of their picnic items away in baskets and crates. All but a few had taken their leave. Before the men took the makeshift table apart and carried the sawhorses away, Tillie turned and poured two cups of coffee.

"Thank you for praying."

Tillie turned to find Everett standing behind her. She noticed he'd donned his shirt once again, covering his long johns. Tillie handed him one of the coffee mugs. His fingers lingered on hers for a few extra moments as he accepted the steaming brew. At his touch, her breathing became more rapid. Tillie studied his dark brown eyes, looking into their depths. She was too filled with wonder to speak.

Weariness etched its mark across his face. "Would you mind if we sat down?" He led the way over to the steps, and it was then Tillie noticed he was limping.

"Everett, you're hurt."

He shook his head as he lowered himself to the step beside her. "It's nothing. I twisted my foot a bit. It'll be fine." He turned and looked fully into her face. "It won't leave a scar."

His tone held no bitterness. She dropped her gaze to her shoe tops for a moment. "Everett Behr, you are an extraordinary man." She returned her shy glance to him.

He shrugged. "There were a lot of men out searching. I was only one of many. God let me find her."

Tillie sipped her coffee and then ran her finger around the rim of the mug. "I noticed little Susan didn't find you repulsive at all. In fact, she clung to you and didn't want to let go when everyone started shouting."

"Tillie, it was amazing." He reached over and picked up her hand, but he didn't seem to realize he'd done so. Torchlight flickered off his face, highlighting his scars. Awe filled his expression, as if he was relating a miracle. "The moonlight came and went as the clouds moved, but when I heard her crying, it was as if God flooded the area with light." He waved his hand, gesturing toward the torches. "The moon was brighter than it had been the entire evening. She looked up at me and climbed right into my arms. She wasn't afraid at all."

"Mm, she thought you were an angel." The smile that began in the depths of her heart grew and rose to fill her entire being. "Everett, your scars are the result of an entirely selfless, love-filled act. Remember, Jesus bore scars from an ultimate act of love. By His scars, we have the hope of heaven. Scars aren't ugly, Everett." She tightened her fingers around his, pulling them toward her. He glanced down at their joined hands and returned the squeeze. When his gaze rose back to meet hers, he lifted his other hand and ran his fingertips over his scars.

Tillie reached out and gently took his hand, pulling it away from his face. "Your scars are beautiful to me."

❧

The warmth permeating Everett's being wasn't the result of sipping the hot coffee. Tillie's nearness quickened his pulse and deepened each breath. The autumn wind sighed through the cedars and flickered the torchlight into ripples across the churchyard. The weariness that had dogged him as he'd made his way through the darkness with little Susan vanished, replaced by revived freshness in Tillie's company. He wanted to stare at her, to take in every nuance of her image and forever commit this moment to memory. She stole his very breath. There was so much he wanted—no, *needed* to say to her. Where should he begin?

"Where's Ben?" *Where's Ben!* He groaned within himself and wanted to yank the words back the instant they escaped. What a stupid thing to say. Where was the comfortable camaraderie they'd enjoyed walking among the willows?

One of her eyebrows arched slightly. "He went out searching with Fletcher Hamilton. They came back a little while ago, after the bell was rung. I don't expect you noticed them in all the commotion."

He hadn't. He only had eyes for Tillie. Another wagon pulled out of the churchyard, its occupants calling out their good nights to the men disassembling the tables and the women finishing the cleanup. He raised his hand to wave in response but quickly returned his focus on Tillie and the moment God was allowing them to share.

Tillie's soft voice intertwined with the song of the night wind. "Ben told me he could see how I felt about you, and he said I wouldn't find a finer man than you. And he's right."

"He did? He is?"

Her laugh reminded him of raindrops falling softly on the

fields. Such a sweet sound. But the smile faded from her face, and she lowered her gaze, twisting her fingers into a knot. "I have to ask you something."

He reached over and disentangled her fingers, holding them gently within his. "You can ask me anything."

She took a deep breath, as if the question on her lips needed a push. "Everett, are you planning on leaving?"

Her inquiry so startled him that he tightened his grip on her hands lest they slip from his grasp. Did she know about the letter? Before he could tell her all the things his heart wanted to say, he needed to begin by being honest.

"I've received an offer of a position back east. How did you know?"

She lifted her shoulders. "My brother Phillip was at work in your father's store. He overheard your father and Miss Pearl talking about you moving back to Baltimore. Phillip said he didn't think your parents knew he was in the storeroom." A tiny smile pulled a dimple into her cheek. "Even though he's my younger brother, he thinks he has to protect me. He didn't mean any harm." The smile fell away. "He told me he heard your parents praying that God would work it out for you to stay in Willow Creek." Her green eyes filled with pain, and she repeated her question. "So are you planning on leaving?"

She pulled one hand away to push back her hair, but Everett held the other one captive. "Honestly? I haven't decided yet. I only received the letter a week ago, and it caught me by surprise. I will admit that I've been thinking about it. In the past couple of weeks, I've found it harder than I believed possible to watch you and Ben together."

"But you were the one who kept telling me I should accept Ben's attention."

Everett pursed his lips and nodded. "I know. I truly

believed I was doing the right thing. These scars. . . How could I expect. . . ? Tillie, I never meant to hurt you. My only thought was to see you happy. I couldn't ask you to spend your life with someone who looks like a freak."

"You stop right there, Everett Behr." A stubborn scowl took up residence on her beautiful face. "I never want to hear you utter those words again." She pulled her hand away from him and plunked both hands on her hips. "You haven't answered my question."

"Yes, I did. I said I haven't decided yet."

She rolled her eyes heavenward. "Angels preserve us!" Those crystal green eyes returned to earth and nailed him where he sat. "Don't you think it's high time you *do* decide? Because I have something I want to say to you, but not until I know if you're planning on staying or leaving."

A bubble of laughter formed in his belly and rose into his chest. He clamped his lips shut. Something told him he'd best hold it in. If the feisty expression on her face was any indication, she might not take it kindly if he laughed.

He sucked in a breath. "I was seriously considering the offer, but circumstances have changed, and it appears God wants me to stay where I am."

The light from the torches burned a bit lower. They'd need to say good night soon. Only two men remained at the church, loading up the last of the sawhorses and planks.

The stubborn look in her eye waned like the torchlight. "What circumstances have changed?"

He reached over and hooked the errant lock of hair back behind her ear once again, his fingers grazing the side of her face. Her soft smile invited his hand to linger there as she tipped her head to nestle into his palm. His rib cage prevented his heart from soaring out of his chest. Sorrow pinched him when he removed his hand from her face.

"God has broken through this thick head of mine and shown me how foolish I've been." How should he explain the dawn of understanding? "For months I told myself the friendship you offered me was simply because of your compassion, and I didn't want anyone feeling sorry for me. Especially you."

She opened her mouth, an expression of protest on her face, but he laid his finger on her lips. Complete honesty demanded he finish his explanation.

"I couldn't see myself asking you to be with someone who looked like me. I truly believed I was sparing you from a lifetime of pain."

He captured her hand again. "Tillie, God has shown me your heart. He's allowed me to glimpse the pure, unspoiled love you have to share." He lifted her fingers to his lips. "Once God pulled the blindfold from my eyes and I understood the depth of your feelings, all those excuses I kept calling reasons fell away."

She reached across the space that separated them and touched his scars, a tiny smile tipping the corners of her mouth. "This is the face I want to see every morning for the rest of my life."

His heart leapt with a freedom he'd never known before, and he couldn't keep the grin from stretching across his face. "Why, Tillie O'Dell, are you asking me to marry you?"

The cockiness he'd come to adore danced in her sparkling eyes. "Unless you ask me first, yes."

Laughter rose up from the delight in his heart and spilled over. "Well, in that case, I accept. But just to make it conventional. . ." He slid off the church step and lowered himself to one knee, taking her hand in his. The flickering light of the torch played over her face and reflected off her eyes. "Tillie, I love you. I've loved you for months and didn't realize it. With God's help, I plan to love you until the day He takes me home. I believe you are the partner He has ordained for me, and I for you. Will you marry me?"

Tillie leaned forward and framed his face with her hands. "I've always wanted my very own angel, and now God has sent me one. . .named Ever."

epilogue

Willow Creek, Iowa, 1887

"Oh, Everett, it's beautiful." Tillie ran her fingers over the pattern of leaded glass in the front door of the house they were building. Sunlight caught the beveled edges of the intricate design. "But isn't it too costly?"

Everett squeezed his wife's shoulders. "Tillie, my love, you are so easy to please, and you never ask for anything. I wanted you to have a little touch of extravagance." He took her hand and led her up the newly painted steps to the wide front porch. "Father has ordered some rocking chairs from a furniture maker in Ohio. I thought we could set them here on the porch and watch the sunset in the evenings."

Tillie smiled up at him. "Sunset always was your favorite time of day." She walked to one end of the porch where a willow tree draped its curtain across the corner of the railing, close enough to reach out and weave her fingers through the dangling green withes. When Everett had shown her the parcel of land at the edge of town that he wanted to purchase, she'd immediately fallen in love with the two willow trees that stood silently beckoning an invitation to hide away in their curtained sanctuaries. Everett had agreed their house should be built right in between them—a giant willow at each end of the sprawling porch.

Tillie smiled and glanced at her husband over her shoulder. "Do you remember how we used to walk in the evenings and watch the fireflies play hide-and-seek through the willow trees?"

Everett's teasing chuckle made her heart flutter. "I seem to recall you taking off your shoes and stockings and dangling your feet in the creek."

A warm blush filled Tillie's face despite the fact they'd been married for almost two years. "How scandalous!"

Everett grinned. "I couldn't see your ankles. Between the twilight and the shadows from the willow trees, it was too dark."

Tillie filled her eyes with the sight of their new house, almost ready for them to move in. "I still can't believe you've had this house built for us. Don't misunderstand—I love the house. It's beautiful, but I'd have been happy living in the apartment over your father's store."

"So you've told me." He placed a gentle kiss on her lips. "I wanted to give you a house of your own. A place where we could grow and establish our own family traditions and memories, a refuge to come home to and a haven for our children. . .someday."

Tillie dipped her head and smiled a private smile over the secret she shared with the Lord. She laid her hand over her abdomen, awe filling her over the tiny life that grew there in its wondrous hiding place. Perhaps this was a good time to tell Everett her news.

"I saw Tessa and Susan today. Susan wanted to know if Uncle Ever was coming to her birthday party."

Everett inspected the framing around the front windows. "She's having another birthday? She must be. . .what, four?"

"She's going to be five years old this Saturday."

"Time sure flies."

"Mm. She's going to be a big sister soon, too. Gideon and Tessa are expecting again."

Everett's face lit up. "That's wonderful. I'll remember to congratulate Gideon when I see him." He laid his hand on the small of her back. "Come on, let's go see how the new kitchen is coming along. Fred Cummings does excellent cabinetry work."

Tillie allowed him to lead her to the front door. "I'm more anxious to see the upstairs."

Everett paused with his hand on the doorknob. "I thought we agreed to wait and finish the upstairs later."

"I believe we said. . .as the need arises."

"Well, yes, but—" Everett's eyes widened.

"Didn't you say there would be enough room for two large bedrooms upstairs?"

"Yes, but—"

"Of course, the room doesn't have to be ready right away. We can wait. . .five, maybe six months."

"But—"

"Won't it be fun for Gideon and Tessa's new baby to have a playmate the same age?"

Her husband stood with his feet anchored in place as he stared unblinking at her.

Tillie gave him her sweetest smile and slid her arms around his neck. "You're going to be a wonderful papa." She watched an expression of absolute rapture sweep across his face.

"Oh, my sweet Tillie." He held her face in both hands and lowered his lips to hers. He pulled his head back and smoothed his fingers over her hair, then raised his eyes to heaven. "Lord, what a marvelous gift You've given us. Every gift from You is perfect. Thank You, Father."

He kissed her again until she was breathless and then wrapped her in his arms. "I can't wait to hold him."

"Him? You know it could be a girl."

Everett blew out his breath tentatively, as if trying not to break the sweet spell of awestruck joy. "A little girl."

She giggled at the look of wonder in her husband's eyes and snuggled into his embrace. A moment later, she found herself scooped up into Everett's arms. Joyous laughter bubbled out of both of them as Everett whooped and whirled her around.

He set her down carefully and grabbed her hand, tugging her down the steps. "Come on!"

"I thought you wanted to look at the house and see how the kitchen was turning out."

"At a time like this? Are you crazy, woman?" He helped her climb into the buggy. "I can't wait to see the expressions on my father's and Pearl's faces when we tell them they're going to be grandparents!"

Pure bliss found expression in her laugh. "My da will do an Irish jig all the way down the main street." She pictured her father's reaction and exclaimed at the image. "Mercy!"

Everett climbed up beside her and unwound the reins from the brake lever. He paused before releasing the brake and pulled her into a tight hug. "Tillie, I love you so much. You are exactly right. God has certainly poured out His mercy on us!"

"Aye," she whispered, adopting her father's vernacular. "His mercy and blessings and love and faithfulness and grace and—"

Everett silenced her list with a kiss.

A Letter To Our Readers

Dear Reader:

In order that we might better contribute to your reading enjoyment, we would appreciate your taking a few minutes to respond to the following questions. We welcome your comments and read each form and letter we receive. When completed, please return to the following:

Fiction Editor
Heartsong Presents
PO Box 719
Uhrichsville, Ohio 44683

1. Did you enjoy reading *Scars of Mercy* by Connie Stevens?
   ❏ Very much! I would like to see more books by this author!
   ❏ Moderately. I would have enjoyed it more if

   _____

   _____

   _____

2. Are you a member of **Heartsong Presents**? ❏ Yes ❏ No
   If no, where did you purchase this book? _____

   _____

3. How would you rate, on a scale from 1 (poor) to 5 (superior), the cover design? _____

4. On a scale from 1 (poor) to 10 (superior), please rate the following elements.

   _____ Heroine   _____ Plot
   _____ Hero   _____ Inspirational theme
   _____ Setting   _____ Secondary characters

5. These characters were special because? _____

_____

_____

6. How has this book inspired your life? _____

_____

_____

7. What settings would you like to see covered in future **Heartsong Presents** books? _____

_____

_____

8. What are some inspirational themes you would like to see treated in future books? _____

_____

_____

9. Would you be interested in reading other **Heartsong Presents** titles? ❑ Yes ❑ No

10. Please check your age range:

❑ Under 18 ❑ 18-24

❑ 25-34 ❑ 35-45

❑ 46-55 ❑ Over 55

Name _____

Occupation _____

Address _____

City, State, Zip_____

E-mail _____

Presents

Great Inspirational Romance
at a Great Price!

Heartsong Presents books are inspirational romances in contemporary and historical settings, designed to give you an enjoyable, spirit-lifting reading experience. You can choose wonderfully written titles from some of today's best authors like Wanda E. Brunstetter, Mary Connealy, Susan Page Davis, Cathy Marie Hake, Joyce Livingston, and many others.

When ordering quantities less than six, above titles are $3.99 each.
Not all titles may be available at time of order.

HEARTSONG
PRESENTS

If you love Christian romance...

$12.⁹⁹

You'll love Heartsong Presents' inspiring and faith-filled romances by today's very best Christian authors...Wanda E. Brunstetter, Mary Connealy, Susan Page Davis, Cathy Marie Hake, and Joyce Livingston, to mention a few!

When you join Heartsong Presents, you'll enjoy four brand-new, mass-market, 176-page books—two contemporary and two historical—that will build you up in your faith when you discover God's role in every relationship you read about!

Imagine...four new romances every four weeks—with men and women like you who long to meet the one God has chosen as the love of their lives...all for the low price of $12.99 postpaid.

Mass Market 176 Pages

To join, simply visit www.heartsong presents.com or complete the coupon below and mail it to the address provided.

YES! Sign me up for Heart♥ng!

NEW MEMBERSHIPS WILL BE SHIPPED IMMEDIATELY!
Send no money now. We'll bill you only $12.99 postpaid with your first shipment of four books. Or for faster action, call 1-740-922-7280.

NAME _____

ADDRESS _____

CITY _____ STATE _____ ZIP _____

MAIL TO: HEARTSONG PRESENTS, P.O. Box 721, Uhrichsville, Ohio 44683
or sign up at WWW.HEARTSONGPRESENTS.COM